'Secrets of Happiness unfolds across families and lovers,

We hope you enjoy this book. Please return or renew it by the due date.

You can renew it at www.norfolk.gov.uk/libraries or by using our free library app.

Otherwise you can phone 0344 800 8020 - please have your library card and PIN ready.

You can sign up for email reminders too.

'A new novel in stories from the master of the form... [E]
choes the great Grace Paley, to whom Silber is so close in
spirit and voice. While Paley was an all-New York gal, Silber makes faraway places seem familiar – oh, for the time
when we can work on knowing the world even one-tenth
as well as she does. These secrets of happiness really will
make you happy, at least for a few sweet hours'

Kirkus Reviews

'Silber's brilliantly realised bird's-eye view has shown us...
[the] people we are connected to are crucial to our happiness, just as we are to theirs' *Irish Times*

'*Secrets of Happiness* is a swim in cool, clear water in which
the contours and colours of all experience are magnified,
purified, intensified. Joan Silber's translucent, morally
attentive prose does something to the vision as well as
the spirit: if you can look up from it, you'll find your own
world altered – rinsed clean, and luminous'

Charlotte Wood

'Few make fiction feel as exciting as Silber – and not in
plot, but mere structure. Characters impact one another.
Tones shift with perspective. Scenes build with profound
scope... This latest novel feels like vintage Silber: stories
interlinked with the confidence of Elizabeth Strout, but all
their own mood and power' *Entertainment Weekly*

'As usual, with *Secrets of Happiness* the magnificent Joan
Silber manages to make great writing look absolutely effortless. A warm, smart, seductive, hugely satisfying novel'

Sarah Waters

'If E.M. Forster hadn't already scooped up "Only connect" as the epigraph for his novel *Howards End*, Joan Silber would have the perfect fit for it. In fact, Silber deserves it a little more… Silber's knack for inhabiting far-flung realities is remarkable… *Secrets of Happiness* pays the best kind of attention to its characters' desires, dilemmas and, of course, connections'
Seattle Times

'The author of the award-winning *Improvement* once again takes her scalpel to the complex anatomy of family, dissecting, with stunning precision, one young New Yorker's struggles with his father's secret life, the toll of deceits that doom a marriage, and the pitfalls of his own sexuality'
O, The Oprah Magazine

'I never wonder more at how little we know about how greatly we factor in other people's lives than I do when reading Silber at her best. She aims, in increments, at the ecstatic… Capable of ecstasy, this time Silber delivers merely something humane, elegant and wise'
Joshua Ferris, **New York Times Book Review**

'These stories are all about small, individual lives lived intensely, joyfully, painfully, successfully, until intersecting planes of time catch up and everyone and everything dissolves into atoms, splitting and splitting again until they are nothing. Silber has a power that the rarest old masters have: close up, you feel their breath breathing life, nothing less, across a rosy cheek. You hold your own breath in those suspended seconds'
The Monthly

'*Secrets of Happiness* is classic Joan Silber … Silber's effortless dissemination of facts in narrative is always impressive because her characters are so engaging and believable'
Susan Straight, **Los Angeles Times**

ALSO BY JOAN SILBER

FICTION

Improvement

Fools

The Size of the World

Ideas of Heaven

Household Words

Lucky Us

In My Other Life

In the City

NONFICTION

The Art of Time in Fiction

Secrets

of

Happiness

Joan Silber

ALLEN&UNWIN

First published in hardback in Great Britain in 2021 by Allen & Unwin

This paperback edition first published in Great Britain in 2022
by Allen & Unwin

First published in the United States in 2021 by Counterpoint

Allen & Unwin
c/o Atlantic Books
Ormond House
26–27 Boswell Street
London WC1N 3JZ

Phone: 020 7269 1610

Email: UK@allenandunwin.com

Web: www.allenandunwin.com/uk

A CIP catalogue record for this book is available from the British Library.

Internal design by Wah-Ming Chang

Paperback ISBN 978 1 91163 009 8
E-Book ISBN 978 1 76063 727 9

Printed and bound in Great Britain by Clays Ltd, Elcograf S.p.A.

10 9 8 7 6 5 4 3 2 1

For Diane Churchill

Secrets

of

Happiness

1 / Ethan

My father was on the road a lot when I was growing up, off to parts of Asia to oversee the cheap manufacture of ladies' garments. You couldn't stay still, he said, in today's business world. "Ever ask him about the local babes?" one of my friends wanted to know. "You should go with him next time, Ethan." He was just being a smart-ass—we were fifteen-year-old boys at the time, obnoxious whenever we could be.

My father complained about too much time away from home—he missed us, he missed New York—and always came back with great presents. My mother and my sister got silk scarves and pearl necklaces. As a first grader I had a kung fu T-shirt from Hong Kong and as a teen I had crazy pop tapes from Thailand. Mike, my friend, tried to get me to gamble away my tapes to him in a card game.

In fact, I had a crush on Mike, a skinny loudmouth guy who was actually quite brainy and who had similar tastes in music. He was not my first crush, but I was still keeping those things to myself. It was the late 1980s, which were

3

not as free as people like to remember. I lived in a world of heated imaginings, a long inner movie with a cast of highly appreciative lovers culled from real life, rock 'n' roll, TV, anything. It was a happier world, of course, than any I ever really entered. I wasn't out till my first year of college.

In high school everybody liked to hang around our apartment. It was homey and messy, with sprawling rooms, very Upper West Side, and big for Manhattan. My mother left us alone—she taught school all day, she didn't need to see kids every minute—and then she'd burst forth at dinner, taking an interest, asking my friends the very questions they wanted to answer. Mike told her he believed in reincarnation, which I didn't even know. And my mother loved parties. When my father came home from a trip, she'd get all my friends to sing some goofy version of "Love Shack," she'd have sparklers flaming away in a platter of pasta. "Where am I?" my father said. "Is this the right house?" He kept his arm around my mother's waist, beamed at all of us. My sister had to tell him every single thing she'd done in school. "Home is the sailor," my mother said, "home from sea. And the hunter home from the hill."

My mother was always hoping to get to travel with him— maybe in the summer, when she was off from teaching?— but he avoided going when it was so hot over there. Over the years his destinations shifted, as American outsourcing shifted, in what he still called the rag trade. First, when I was

4

little, it was Hong Kong and then it seemed to be Thailand and Malaysia and Indonesia, and later China and Bangladesh. "Every country is different," he said. My sister used to ask him about the languages—he could say *hello* and *thank you* in Cantonese; Thai; Bahasa Malaysia, which was almost the same as Bahasa Indonesia; Mandarin, and Bangla. "Only *hello* and *thank you*? That's all?" my sister said.

"Also *delicious* and *very good*," he said. "People speak English, they have to. They know we're idiots."

Sometimes he took us to a favorite Thai restaurant in Queens, out in Elmhurst, where he traded a few phrases with the hostess, who always gave us a good table. The food was vastly better than any namby-pamby Thai food in Manhattan and we bragged about it to our friends.

My mother always meant to learn more about the textiles, which she was a big fan of, from getting all those scarves. And all the religions! Buddhists, Taoists, Communists, Muslims. "Asia is fascinating," my father said, happy capitalist exploiter that he was. When his company merged with a bigger outfit, he bragged about making more money, but it was all the same to us.

I waited till he was home, during spring vacation of my freshman year, to break the news to both of them that my new love interest was someone named Robert. They were okay about it, pretty much. Well, my mother was better. And I swore to her I always, always took precautions. My father said, "I have to revise everything I know."

"Not everything," I said.

Robert and I later had jokes about the radical changes my father might see in me—acute skin pallor from lack of sleep, cheerful expression from lots of sex, tighter pants from being so sexy. But Robert liked my parents when he met them. I brought him back from Yale at the end of the semester, just for a quick visit. My mom made a perfect roast chicken and got him explaining his paper on Thoreau. What he said about them was, "They're so lively. A lot of people's parents seem depressed to me but not yours."

How romantic I was in those days. I remembered things Robert said as if they were words to a book I was learning by heart. I might have had all his passing phrases tattooed on my skin, I went over them so often (I didn't yet mind repetition). Of course, I had my own intricate opinions about the world, and we had long, elating discussions; we hardly knew what we meant and we went on in great obscure delight. We were really very well-matched—who knew?—and it was clearer to me every day that this new life I had was my best life. Robert had more experience but he too was swept away. We studied at the same table in the library; we ate at chairs across from each other in the dining hall. Kevin, one of our friends, said, "You're so codependent, it's cute."

People like Kevin were the problem. There was a fad, after a while, of making fun of our devotion—"here come the lovebirds"—and under these quips I looked bad, the puppy-dog lover. Robert was better at making snarky remarks back—"I feel so sorry for my little single friends"—while I blanched and practically sniffled. I wasn't used to anything. These were gay men attacking me, how could this be? "They're kidding," Robert said. "Ever hear of humor?"

Weren't we meant to band together, knowing what we knew all too well about the virus that wanted to kill us? I was more used to the dread than I'd once been (now that there was no turning back), but was I wrong to think of all of us as warriors together? "Hey, that's what armies are like," Robert said.

All the same, we lasted a full year and a half as a couple, a fairly long time at that stage of life, and we weren't even that angry when we ended it. But we kept running into each other every time we walked across campus, and sometimes the sight of him stabbed me to the core. My mother said, "Assume a virtue if you have it not. Act cool, that's all." She was a great help to me at this time, in her way.

I always thought my mother must be an outstanding teacher. You'd set out on a basic, simple path and she'd lead you to dizzying heights so you thought you'd gotten there of your own accord. All the years she taught eighth-grade English at a middle school in the Bronx did not make her hate rereading *The Old Man and the Sea* or *The Autobiography of Miss Jane Pittman* or *A Tale of Two Cities* or Langston Hughes or Emily Dickinson. When I was little, she used to read me Hughes's "Hold fast to dreams," and I'd recite the lines to my much more sophisticated self when I was older and having a hard time.

Men gave me trouble. Over and over. My sister, Allyson, said, "Men give everyone trouble. They're no good."

I did see a future of recurrent doom. I was in my last year of law school then at NYU—people say they have no time to date in law school, but I'd managed to charm my way into any number of disastrous relationships. People abandoned me, they insulted me, they borrowed money, they disappointed me by being stupid. And none of it was carefree fun. My father gave me lectures on avoiding the virus at all costs—I was careful, wasn't I? We lived under a shadow in those days, everyone's forgotten already. My meanest boyfriend died three years after I knew him.

My sister, who became beautiful once she grew into her nose and teeth, was also bad at picking partners. A freeloading actor, a braggadocio journalist, a chef who turned out to be married. I thought it was a family curse (people with worse parents than mine did fine, what was the problem?) until she turned up one Thanksgiving with Blake, a college friend now turned boyfriend, just finishing his residency in pediatrics, who was forthright and modest and dryly hilarious and seemed to dote on her. They were married at the Cloisters; I didn't even know you could do that. My mother, very festive in a flashy brocade tunic my father had brought from somewhere, kept saying, "This is what makes a mother happy." We all got plastered, of course, and over the hors d'oeuvres table I had a riotous discussion with some dude about how they got the pimientos in the olives. His name was Tony and he wasn't bad-looking either.

I fell in love at my sister's wedding. What could be sillier than that? He was a lawyer too, it turned out, and he was the most like me of anyone I'd dated since Robert the freshman. Like me if I were less anxious and more handsome. We tried to pace ourselves and we'd been together almost a year before we looked for an apartment.

We had just moved in together and were still arranging the furniture this way and that, seeking the perfection we knew was ours, in a happy sort of dither, when I got the phone call from my sister. "It's about Dad, and you're not going to believe this."

I was thinking, *If it's cancer, Blake will know who he should see*, but it wasn't that. My mother had come home from school to find a legal notice slid under the door, informing my father that he was named in a paternity petition. The petitioner had a long multisyllabic name my sister couldn't remember and there were two male children she was making claims for, aged fifteen and seventeen. Fifteen and seventeen! They resided in Woodside, New York.

"Holy fuck," I said.

"Mom thought maybe it was a mistake," Allyson said. "You know, they got the name wrong. But it's not a mistake."

My father had a whole other family. The suit said so and my father said so too, once he had to say something. He explained that the woman was from Thailand, he'd brought her over and given her and the kids (both born here) a good life, but for some people nothing was ever enough. He was very sorry a certain individual was being this way and that my mother had to go through this.

My mother kept saying, "I feel crazy." She'd been married to the man for thirty-two years. "I just feel crazy," she said, then and later. She did have the presence of mind to tell him he had to move out immediately and she got him to believe her. "Married thirty-two years," she said. To anyone who would listen.

My sister thought my mother should have known. How could she not have? "Why are you blaming the victim?" I said. My sister the bride—she must've wanted to see my mother as much more shockingly dumb than she would ever be.

We all had to think differently about my father, who

had lived for so many years with his secret. He must have liked the power of it (he liked power). *Guess what I know and you don't.* The woman, he let us know, was the hostess at the Thai restaurant we liked in Queens. I didn't even really remember what she looked like, I'd been too focused on the barbecued chicken with sticky rice, but what a thing to do to her.

My father, who acted much put upon by all the fuss, rented a furnished studio apartment in the West Fifties that was like a hotel room. He apparently wasn't in any hurry to move in with his other family—well, the woman was suing him, wasn't she? "Women always want money," he told me, when I went to visit him. "You're lucky you're not involved with women."

"Mom was never a gold-digger," I said. He had given me a glass of bourbon and we were sitting around his rented glass coffee table.

"I don't say anything against your mom," he said. There was a pause, while we both thought of what she had to say against him, as loudly as she could. *My husband buried me in bullshit and laughed about it.*

"Can I ask you for some legal advice?" he said.

"You cannot," I said. There was no end to my father's nerve.

✦ ✦ ✦

I was thinking about *Treasure Island*, my favorite book during preadolescence, which had no females in it, just males of all classes running after silver and gold. But my father was really saying that money had to do with sex. Not for direct payment, he wouldn't mean that, but for showing off, for shining bright, for expecting and taking more— that was what it was good for. My father never stopped carrying himself as a man with a full wallet. And where had it gotten him? We were still finding out.

My boyfriend Tony was concerned about my mother. She was staying home every night, sleeping through the weekends, not answering phone calls, looking like hell. "My marriage was an illusion," she kept saying. "For thirty-two years." Tony thought it was important that we take her to dinner every week. He'd notice what she wore—"just some old thing," she'd say, only half joking—and then he'd talk about something he just read, and he could get her going, comparing writers, dishing the bad ones, sounding like herself. "Maybe I should retire," she said. "I always dreamed of having nothing to do but read." She was only fifty-six and we both thought this was a terrible idea. No matter how much cash she got in the divorce settlement.

"What else did you dream of, Abby?" Tony said.

Was he her therapist? But she liked the question. "My

esteemed husband, Gil, got to do all the traveling," she said. "I always wanted to travel. Well, we know why he never took me."

"You should go," Tony said. "No time like the present."

She took it to heart, this bit of free advice. However, instead of the Louvre and the Prado or Stratford-upon-Avon and the Cotswolds, she wanted to go to Asia—well, she'd been hearing about it for years. She really thought she'd go see Thailand—everyone said it was such a beautiful country. *What? Thailand?* How could she be so weirdly unoriginal, so blatantly ironic? "Well, I'm not going to Bangkok, where your father always went," she said. "I'd go to the north, to Chiang Mai. You don't even know where that is, do you?" I didn't.

She thought she'd probably go for a year. Even Tony said, "A year? What will you do?"

"Teach English," my mother said. "I've signed up for it already."

My sister thought our mom was acting like some student backpacker. "Every dropout gives English lessons." Meanwhile, my mother went about subletting the big apartment for a fat monthly fee. "Someone else is going to live in our house!" my sister said. My mother said someone we didn't know had been living in it for years, meaning our father.

"It's so interesting what travel does," Tony said. "Look how much courage she suddenly has to go off into the unknown."

"She's not there yet," I said, but I was impressed by the way my mother was now taking charge of her fate. She bought a rain jacket and walking sandals; she got vaccines for hepatitis and pills for malaria. She read *Lonely Planet Thailand* and *Fodor's*; she listened to *Pimsleur Thai*. "Do you know the language has five tones?" she told me. I thought my mother had found a way not to be bitter.

She sent an email to say she'd arrived safely—*writing you from a very nice cybercafe with delicious snacks*—and then we didn't hear from her for two weeks. Her next notes were brief. *Lots of rain in September, water never hurt anyone. Students not used to speaking up but I am nagging them. Trying not to mind rain on walks. Miss our dinners very much.*

"She must be lonely," Tony said. The other teachers were young, she said, and none of them were (by her standards) big readers. I wondered if she had anyone to lament to about her rotten husband, Gil. Or maybe her coworkers were fleeing her laments.

But then something changed, as it does with travelers.

The messages had bits of bragging in them, words in Thai, signs of familiarity with local whatnot. "Hard work but time is going by," my mother said. "Of course, we're on a different clock here. I don't think I can explain."

Tony mentioned going to visit her over New Year's (Chiang Mai was so fun-loving it celebrated three different new year's, including ours), but I had to admit, I didn't want to spend my vacation time with my mother. "She's becoming her other self," I said. "She doesn't need us." Tony gave me a look of high disapproval. Well, it wasn't his mother.

Her messages, though few and far between, had brighter particulars now. She was apparently hanging out with the couple who ran the school and she had Thai friends too. My sister wondered if maybe she was seeing a guy, that was why she was forgetting us, but I didn't think so. Neither did Tony. There's a smug triumph that always seeps into the tone of a love-struck person's correspondence and my mother's didn't sound like that. She was happy from other things—the fabric she found at the night market, the celebration at the temple on the mountain, and the trek in the forest she and her friends did one weekend, where they saw caves and waterfalls.

None of us wasted time worrying about my father. If he minded being on his own, if he minded paying out money to two different women, neither of whom took care of him, it was his own fucking fault. When I spoke to him, he complained of how much harder it was to do business in China. My sympathy on the topic was thin.

My sister said, "I think he's dyeing his hair. Isn't that ridiculous?"

"How young could he look?" I said. "He's sixty-two." In truth he was still a very decent-looking man.

My sister was the one who got called by a nurse at Roosevelt Hospital, after my father couldn't get up from the table at his favorite diner and the waiter tried to help him and it turned out he'd had a stroke. Allyson was weepy when she phoned me. How bad was it? Bad enough. "His speech is slurred but you can understand him. He's very confused," she said. "He thinks he's in Beijing. We should call Mom, we have to get her home."

By the time we got hold of my mother, the prognosis for my father was somewhat better. He'd stay for more tests, he'd be put on a whole regimen of drugs, and with proper rest at home most of his symptoms would lift. "He's not in pain?" my mother said. Her voice was shaking.

"No, and I don't think he's in any immediate danger," I said. I wanted to soothe her as well as I could.

"He's not dying," she said, softly.

I went on about what a good hospital it was. My sister's husband thought highly of the doctors. And my father could have a health care aide at home if he needed it, but maybe he wouldn't even need it. Really, the doctors were very optimistic. "You can stay with me and Tony when you come back," I said. "I know the tenants are at your place."

"I'm not coming back," my mother said. "Thank you for letting me know."

I'd never known my mother to be heartless, so what was her heart doing now? "What makes you think he'd be glad to see me?" she said. I was phoning from my office this time, very early in the morning; it was still dark outside the windows.

"It's so obvious he misses you," I said. "He never wanted you to leave, you know that. That wasn't what he had in mind at all."

She laughed at this. "No, it wasn't. He just wanted everything at once. In Thailand the monks say greed is one of the three poisons in life."

"Do they?" I said. I was sort of stuck for an argument. Who could defend greed? Though people did and were paid well for it.

"There was a big full-moon festival last night," my mother said. "Lots of people walking round the temples."

❖ ❖ ❖

"If he gets sicker, do you think she'll come home?" my sister said.

"What makes you think I know?" I said. "And try not to jinx him by saying that."

Our mother had now become a mystery to us. Just when we'd gotten used to our father. She never got a cell phone that worked in Thailand, so we had to arrange to call her at designated times at her school office, to further remind us how far away she was. But she did take it upon herself to phone my father. "Gil, you're such a pill," she said to him (my father told us later). "You have to get better, you're no good at being sick."

My father went for it. "I was always a crappy patient. They wanted to charge me double at the hospital for driving them nuts."

"Try to rest, for Christ's sake," my mother said. He swore he would, just because she asked.

"Very short phone call," my father told us. "Not using up too many nickels."

My sister was hoping that the catastrophe of his stroke was going to bring our parents together again. Did people's children always want that? I wasn't sure I did.

"She's doing so well now," Tony said. "It's inspiring, don't you think?"

I admired her too, but I didn't know that I wanted to be inspired by any stellar methods of getting through a terrible breakup. I wanted to live the rest of my life without having to know this; I hoped to be coupled forever. I watched my mother anyway—how well she was doing without what we expected her to need, how much less she was at the mercy of all of us—and I saw that I was storing away the details for a rainy day or whatever.

My mother came back from Thailand at the end of August, after her full year away. Tony and I picked her up at the airport. She was dressed like the proverbial backpacker my sister said she was, in sandals and jeans, beads around her neck. She'd gotten a good settlement in the divorce, but you never would've known. "Hello, you two!" she said, throwing her arms around both of us at once. "I'm so glad to see you!"

It was hot as blazes in the parking lot and we apologized for the long walk to our car. "Heat doesn't kill you," she said. "People complain about nothing." She was the mom of my youth, but Tony had hardly ever seen her like this before.

The tenants had paid for a thorough cleaning, and when we got her to the apartment, the rooms were like a stage set. "I forgot all this," she said, as we were walking through the door.

"That's because it looks so clean," I said.

"What a big apartment," she said, as if she really had forgotten.

She didn't want to have dinner with us that night, though we'd booked a table at an expensive Tuscan place she always liked. "You need their panzanella," Tony said.

"I need empty time now," she said.

My mom and Tony were never quite on the same footing again. They were still very fond, but she was more opinionated now, less eager to be directed, and she had a new disdain for trendy eateries with well-dressed crowds. She went back to her old job, which she seemed to like fine, but she did keep saying the kids were so different. "Different how?" I said.

"They have so much to say," she said. "They argue with me. It's not bad."

She and my father had no contact with each other, as far as any of us knew. He was back on the road again, bringing home bolts of silk and handcrafted clay pots from his visits to Dhaka. (Did we know it was the capital of Bangladesh? Now we did.) He had theories about the new China, if we wanted to listen. Very complicated business climate. My sister said, "He's so boring now. Was he always this boring?"

"Mom did more of the talking. We didn't even see him that much."

"He's like some unbearable old guy you meet at a party who can only talk about himself and doesn't even notice that you're not listening."

"I bet he's the same as ever," I said. "Kids don't have a real view of their parents."

"He's worse," she said. "I really think he is."

Meanwhile my mother was talking about wanting to go to Iceland to see the northern lights. You had to go in winter and you could miss them if the weather wasn't right. But wouldn't it be great to see those colors?

"Look what you started her on," I said to Tony. "Now she thinks the world is her oyster."

"She's the Merry Widow," Tony said. "Freed by single-hood." It was hard to think of my mother in one of those lace-up brassieres Merry Widows always wore. "Maybe she'll come back with a Norseman," Tony said.

I didn't think so, but it had already been proven several times over that I didn't know anything.

My mother ended up not going that winter, but she did a project with her eighth graders about Norse sagas, tales of Odin with his wolf and raven companions and Thor with his hammer and Loki the shape-shifter. The unit was a big hit. She got them listening to alliteration in Old Norse, how cool was that. "I'm having such a good time with it," she said.

She'd always been curious but now she had extra scope, practice in gazing farther. Tony thought that we ourselves should go somewhere soon, we never went anywhere. What about Tokyo? Neither of us had ever been to Japan. I didn't know if I was ready, strange language, unreadable writing, raw puffer fish that could kill you in sashimi, but I acted as if the idea showed once again how brilliant he was.

In April, when my father was in Dhaka, seeing about another factory, he collapsed in the heat one afternoon. "What was he doing walking around in that heat?" my sister said. Someone from his company had him driven to a hospital, and the doctors there thought he'd probably had another stroke but weren't entirely sure. My sister got hold of his New York doctor, who arranged to have him flown home.

When we went to see him in the hospital in New York, he did seem more confused this time. He knew me and my sister—"the brats are here!"—but he wasn't sure who Blake was, and he was entirely puzzled about my having a boyfriend and smirked as if we were kidding him. His fuzzy diction got clearer as we stayed, and he asked us to bring him a kind of pretzels he liked. He knew the brand but it took him a minute to find the word *pretzel*.

I did the next visit by myself, and he had a baseball game on the TV, which he probably talked about more coherently than I did. "You should play more sports, Ethan," he said. "It would help you." I didn't stay long.

It was hard to get a straight story on how long they planned to keep him. My sister did the next visit, and when she got to his room, the bed was empty. Maybe they'd moved him, they never told you anything in these places, but my sister found herself weeping. At the nurses' station, someone read the report on the computer. "Oh, he went home this morning. His family came for him."

"*We're* his family," Allyson said.

They really couldn't say any more. My sister had his cell phone number, she did have that (did the man even have the phone with him?)—she left a message. "Dad! Just let us know!"

"Of course. He's with his *mia noi*," my mother said, when we told her. "His minor wife, that's what they call it. She's probably taking good care of him. Poor girl."

My mother still had the paternity papers, with the woman's name and address on them. If that was still her address, these three years later. She never got a penny out of him either. No landline phone listed; my mother even tried different spellings. "But we *have* to *see* him," my sister said. How many messages could she leave? We were at my mother's apartment then, at the big kitchen table. My sister looked like a harpy, red-eyed and wrecked, and my mother was miserable but steady, with the legal papers in her lap.

When my sister's phone rang, my mother said, "Oh! Oh!" and I said, "That's it!" and it was.

"Okay," my sister was saying. "Yes. Of course. I see. Thank you. Yes."

"It was one of the sons," she told us after. One of our half brothers! My father was doing all right, she was told. He wasn't quite up to talking on the phone. But, yes, we could visit, that would be very nice.

My sister and I went together, the first time. We got a little lost on the way, even though it was a big apartment building on a main street. The woman who answered the door—did I recognize her from the restaurant?—was in her forties, handsome in a plain, unmade-up way. "Hello, you are here, very glad," she said. She didn't look that glad.

Our dad was in the living room, lying on the sofa, sitting up to watch a big TV hung on the wall. "You found me," he said. Why was he watching a cartoon?

My sister leaned down to hug him. "You look good," she lied. At least he was shaved, which the hospital didn't always do.

"I'm not dead," he pointed out. His speech was not the clearest.

"Can I turn down the TV?" I said.

"The what? Yes." He spoke slowly. "Sit down, you can

sit. You want tea? We have tea. Abby, bring them the kind I like. You know. And cookies. My daughter likes cookies."

Abby was my mother's name. My sister gave me a look. The woman, who went for the tea anyway, was called Nok (we knew this), though she had a longer name in the legal papers.

It was an ordinary living room, all beige upholstery and blond wood, bare and neat. This woman had sued him once, demanded money by law for the sons—so had he forked over cash now to convince her to let him move in? Could he even write a check at the moment? Or turn over his bank card, with the password? Probably he could, with coaching.

The woman came back from the kitchen with a pot of tea and cups on a tray. She didn't look crafty or foxy to me. But people who thought they were entitled to something didn't look sneaky. Any lawyer sees that. She hardly spoke while we made efforts to talk to our father. My sister told him about Blake's work in a clinic, very long hours with babies. "Parents can be such a pain," she said. "They still believe this totally discredited theory that vaccines give you autism—it's so crazy." I couldn't tell if my father was following her drift. I piped up with a few words about how nice the weather was getting. He always liked warm weather.

"Excuse me, I'm getting tired," my father said. "That's how I am now. Do you need money, either of you?"

"*What?*" we both said. "*No!*" How insulted we were. "*Dad!*" my sister said.

"Abby will see you out," he said. He did let us hug him goodbye.

I thought that he might leave Queens and go back to his own apartment, once he was better, but he didn't get better. My sister was the one who did most of the visiting. Neither of us got to meet the sons, but Allyson managed to get Nok to say that one was studying computer science and one had gone back to her sister in Thailand. Allyson saw their photos, good-looking boys (the older kid had Dad's chin); Nok seemed desolate about the one who'd left the country. Probably Nok was desolate about much more than we knew.

I took Tony with me on one visit. He was socially much more adept than I was, and he actually had a sort of conversation with my dad about current trade agreements with China. And he explained the subprime mortgage crisis to him, which was just starting to surface then. My father said, "I'm glad you have intelligent friends, not like when you were young."

When we left, Tony said, "He calls her Abby! Are all women the same to him? Why don't you stop him?"

"He never listened to us."

Blake thought that my father had probably had a few

mini-strokes since the last big one. Reading wasn't something he could do anymore. Nok sometimes took him outside, on nice summer days, but he wasn't walking very far.

It was already October when my sister phoned me to say, "Dad seems the same to me, but Blake thinks he's slipping. Do you think Mom wants to see him, while she can?"

I thought that we had to ask her. My mother said, "Oh, dear," in a heartbroken way. Yes, she would go, no question. Definitely, she would go.

I was my mother's escort, and as soon as Nok opened the door, she put her palms together in front of her face and made a little bow to my mother. She never did that to us! My mother just nodded back.

My father was napping on the sofa, breathing with a wheezing noise, when we came into the living room. "Visitors," Nok said, and he jerked up and opened his eyes.

"Hey, Gil," my mother said. "It's me, it's Abby."

"Abby's here," my father said.

"Yes, I am. Right you are."

She sat herself in a chair by the couch. "How are you?"

"I've been better," my father said, with his new slowness. "How are you? How are things on West End Avenue these days?" He did know her.

"Pretty good. I just had the kitchen redone. What a pain."

"How's Geraldo?" That was the super.

"Geraldo retired. Another person does it now."

"Nice guy, Geraldo, but he wasn't the handiest. Maybe this guy is better."

"Not what I heard," my mother said.

Nok, who had slipped off to make tea, was back in the room setting down the tray of cups and a steaming teapot. "You like sugar?" she said to my mother. "I get it if you want."

"Abby *never* takes sugar," my father said. He looked at Nok in outrage. And then he gazed from one woman to the other, his eyes widened, and he pursed his lips. Was he confused, was that it? Or just pissed off?

"You don't know," my mother said. "Maybe I've started taking sugar. People change."

"I didn't mean you," my father said.

Nok was slipping back into the kitchen, a tactful move. "This is a terrific kind of tea," I said to my dad.

"Abby!" he called out. "Don't forget cookies."

"I am not forgetting." Nok emerged from the kitchen doorway with a plate of Oreos.

My mother looked horrified—the name thing was clear now—but she wasn't asking any questions. She sipped her tea in panicked politeness.

My father wasn't drinking out of any teacups—he sucked something through a straw from a plastic beaker, and it shook in his hand. I put it down for him when I thought he was done.

"This fall," my mother said, "I've been disappointed in the autumn leaves. Aren't they much brighter colors most years? I think it isn't cold enough yet."

"It cost money to get them those colors," my father said.

My mother piled all our cups on the tray with the teapot and she got up and carried it into the kitchen, where Nok had retreated. I could hear the water running in the sink. One of them laughed. They seemed to be washing the dishes together.

"Mom always likes to clean up right away," I said, a fact of no interest to him. He was looking at the TV, which wasn't on. How had two such women loved him? We could hear them murmuring in the kitchen. And yet they had both been furious with him once, had hired lawyers to demand his money, filed complaints in enraged language. But here they were, tidying up around the old buzzard, sudsing and rinsing, straightening up. They were doing it out of love and out of something like honor, though he had failed them both in the honor category.

Now my father was slumped to one side, drowsing off, and he hiccupped and gasped as part of his breathing. Alarming to hear, those crackling eruptions, and it did no good to be alarmed. It was time only to be respectful, wasn't it? Even I knew that. When my mother came back into the room, she said, "Guess we bored him to sleep. We'll let him have his little nap."

We thanked Nok in the kitchen. "Nothing to thank," she said. "No thanks."

That visit was my mother's only visit, though my father lasted another eight months. I was never sure if he remembered her being there—he went silent whenever I spoke of it, and I wasn't ready to quiz him about the Abbys of his life.

My mother told me later that Nok had made that little bow to her because she was older. "A lot older," my mother said, wryly.

"She could get all his money," Tony said to me, when we were alone. "This Nok. Leave the rest of you without a dime."

"That is so not the issue," I said.

"You say that now."

Would Tony leave me if someday in the future I was penniless? I had enough pennies at the moment, certainly, but he was a man for whom a certain flair was essential, a level of ease and taste. Or so he thought.

Allyson had by this time met Nok's and my father's older son, Joe, who she said had a cool haircut and was perfectly nice. Joe was the one who called her with the news, early that summer, that our father had just died. "I'm so sorry, you know I'm very sorry," he said. By her account, the conversation was awkward and quite tearful on her side. She kept saying, "So soon?"

Nobody knew what to do with my father's body. Who *was* his family? Within the afternoon (no time to wait) my mother had it sent to a Jewish funeral home (we weren't religious but that was the thing to do), a place Reformed enough to cremate it; no ceremony needed.

The lawyer who'd always been my father's lawyer said that my dad hadn't changed his will in more than twenty years. Of course, there could be another lawyer, a later will. We politely asked Nok for any papers he had left behind. She brought to my apartment a shoebox of receipts and half-paid bills and illegible lists. He'd been at her place for more than a year and that was all she had? Where was his computer? Left at the old apartment in the West Fifties. And everything abandoned there had been tossed out some time ago. Nok was surprised we thought she knew anything. "He was sick," she said. Any traces of him had been erased from his old office in his company as well.

So there it was. All the money (he still had money) went to my mother. "Maybe," my mother said, "he meant to leave it for the other Abby, since he sort of thought we were the same."

It was difficult to tell what he ever thought, but he had certainly been in his right mind at the time he signed the will. "It's okay, Mom," we said.

◆ ◆ ◆

"Maybe he was happiest with my mother," I said to Tony. "Do you think he was?"

"I bet he was happiest," Tony said, "when he first met Nok, and he began a double life that wasn't too complicated yet. I bet he was pleased as punch."

Punch was not my idea of happiness, but it may well have been my dad's.

My mother, in the meantime, wanted to give some of her newly inherited money to a charity in Thailand that helped sustain and protect forest regions; she wanted to donate a nice sum in my father's name, in memory of him.

"What's with this fucking name thing?" I said to Tony. "Let her leave the trees alone. They don't need to hear petty human names."

"Maybe your mother should just get another husband and call him Gil," Tony said. "That would be cheaper."

In our early days Tony had a few instances of calling me Mark, the boyfriend before me. Habits lingered. Did it mean everyone was really the same under the sheets? We all hoped not, didn't we?

I didn't know what Nok expected, but she had left her job at the restaurant to tend to Dad and he certainly wasn't helping with the rent anymore. I sold off some mutual funds and sent her a check—twenty thousand, not a fortune—telling myself it'd get replenished by whatever my mom left me someday. "My father and the rest of us wanted to make sure you get this," I wrote. A bit of a fib, no one wanted it except me, but I didn't want her to think I was paying her off like a hooker. She kept the money.

My sister hated my doing this ("it's against our family"), my mom was pointedly neutral ("it's your dollars"), and the one who was really offended was Tony. He acted as if I were taking it from him, from some fountain of eternal delight that was ours to splash in. "We'll never get to go anywhere," he said. "You don't care."

Spurned for disloyalty on all sides, I had an odd moment of sympathy with my father. I missed him, all of a sudden, as if I hadn't gotten it before then that he really wasn't ever coming back. He wasn't just off in Kuala Lumpur or Jakarta. How hard he must've worked at that elaborate life of his, hiding and emerging and making himself up. He took to his roles, as spies do, but it wasn't the easiest way to live.

The next few years were rocky ones with Tony, but we stuck it out. I was grim and irritable right after my father's death and couldn't stand doing anything but staying home; Tony was having clashes with a partner in his law firm. And then we began gradually to quarrel less, talk less, do everything less. We began to say staleness was natural in the life of a couple. For a few years we had (Tony's idea) a more or less open relationship, which many people said was far better than keeping secrets; I wouldn't recommend it.

We'd been together ten years when we agreed to split up for good. I was forty by then, not the best age to be suddenly single, in my opinion. My mother said, "Plenty of lovely men. All you need is one." Just one: hers was the last generation to believe in long marriages. She'd married my dad in her twenties and only dated a little before. Not like us, carrying around our long histories of wild mistakes, dumb ideas, golden triumphs, ones that got away: our lists.

"You'll find someone," my mother said.

She meant well, but what did she know? She of all people.

Maybe it was time for me to travel. "It takes you out of yourself," my mother said. "Which is a happier state than it sounds."

Of course, my father had gone all over the globe and it hadn't taken him out of anything. He'd expected to go on forever with his two families, delighted with how much he'd grabbed. I bet Nok had another boyfriend by now; I bet everyone had one but me.

Once, when I was growing up, I asked my father if he

really had to be away so much. Other fathers stayed home. "Well," he said, "not everyone is as ambitious as I am. I work my tail off at a business I understand better than most people." I was a teenager and could only think, *Big fucking deal.* He wasn't even super-rich; he was just a blowhard.

"You probably believe someone like you should get two votes in every election," I said.

My father laughed and said, "Yeah, I do."

I'd guessed right, hadn't I? I got spiteful then and said, "Why did you ever want to be a parent?"

"I love children," he said.

He did. He'd roughhoused with us on the floor when we were little, made up songs, taught us dance steps, been charmed by us. He may have been thinking of his other children too, when he said that. They would've been little babies, home with Nok.

In Thailand, my mother had once written to us, in the days when she really liked it there, they had a National Children's Day. Games and events all over; even the army was nice to kids. Why didn't we have such a thing?

Around this time my sister, who had sometimes been more attached to our father than I was, went into a phase of being mad at him for spending too much of his money. She had two kids of her own, a boy and a girl, and there would be less for them, because of what his extra family had cost. My mother thought this was a misguided view. "No one is starving," she said.

This was the right view, wasn't it, don't stuff yourself. My father might have done well to listen. How different the two of them had always been (hadn't they noticed?). Allyson and I were paying a quick Sunday visit to our mother while this discussion went on. "People have to learn what's enough," my mother told us. "You know what they did in Iceland?"

"Not Iceland again," my sister said. My mother was thinking once more about going off to see the northern lights, sometime in winter.

"The country voted twice not to bail out failed banks; they let the currency collapse. People decided to just be less prosperous." The moral was sketchy, but my mother was used to teaching. "Iceland got third place in the World Happiness Report," she said.

"Who scored that test?" my sister said. "A walrus?"

I didn't believe they could measure such a thing. But I could see that my mother now liked imagining the calm and prudent Icelanders, eating their fish and not complaining. Through the sunless winters. "Will you please," she said to me, "tell your sister not to worry?"

2 / Joe

MY HIGH SCHOOL GIRLFRIEND WANTED ME TO marry her. Who gets married in high school?

"My mother isn't even married," I said.

"That's your argument?" Veronica said.

It was very devoted of her, very desperate. She was going off to college in the fall, to Michigan, and I was staying home in Queens, neighborhood guy that I was, and she didn't want to lose me. We had sex whenever we could, that summer before she left, but I didn't make any false promises. I'd be reeking from my job washing dishes at the Golden Treasure Thai Restaurant, and she'd act as if sweat and grease were so seductive she couldn't stand it. All summer we were at it, with melancholy adding deeper pangs to the act. Wherever I was, she was in my head every second, but I knew it couldn't last forever.

And it didn't. We phoned and emailed every day the first month—*miss you, miss you,* we wrote—but then she got busy with school and extra activities they had at night, and I was taking computer courses and still putting in my hours at the restaurant, and right when she had to talk to me about a certain person she met in Cinema Club, he knew amazing things about film, I already had a thing going with a girl in my Intro to Data Structures class. "You know how sorry I am," she said, and she was tearful. My voice was hoarse when I said I was sorry too. Part of me was relieved, but not as relieved as I expected.

"You're better off," my mother said. "Not ready for any weddings."

Veronica married that guy from college, right after graduation, and it turned out his last name was the name of a famous department store. He came from a family with unspeakable sums of money. I never thought that was why she married him—she wasn't like that—and people told me they lived in a junky apartment in Bushwick, before those blocks got so gentrified. I heard he wasn't into showy spending, the husband. He worked as a cameraman, which paid decently when any film wanted him, which wasn't that often. People said he was an okay guy. He would never be okay by me, but that wasn't his fault.

Veronica had not grown up fancy. Her dad was the maintenance supervisor (that meant head janitor) of our elementary school, and her mom stayed home with Veronica and the three other kids. When my younger brother, Jack, who always had behavior issues, decided to scribble with Magic Marker all over the lockers, her father had him wash it all off with a scrub brush and scouring powder, and he got Jack to do it very peaceably. He scared him just enough to convince him.

My mother was always worried about Jack. By the time he was fifteen, he was hanging around with what I called thugs (she had a word in Thai). Queens had plenty of Asian gangs, big on extortion and drugs and territorial brutality, and they had teenage gangs attached to them, like farm teams. Jack was hovering around a mixed cadre of Chinese and Vietnamese guys, not nice people. My mother was frantic to switch him into another school, get him away from those thugs, back to his better self. Mothers had their illusions. And how was she going to do this? Her American lover, our father who didn't live with us, had plenty of money. There were schools that could take my brother in hand.

Our father refused flat out. His American kids, his regular family, had gone to public schools, and they were perfectly fine. He believed in public education. He wasn't paying out an extra thirty thou a year in tuition for my crazy brother. There was no discussing it, as far as he was concerned. They did discuss it, in furious voices, and my mother was so outraged she filed papers against him in court. It cost her money too.

She hadn't known, of course—what did she know?—how long the legal stuff would go on. And there was Jack, not improving, so she moved to plan B. She sent my brother back to Bangkok, to live with her sister. I think he went without protesting because he'd heard Bangkok was wilder than Queens, more full of interesting trouble, and maybe for him it was. He was smiling like a fox in his photos. And in Thailand he was never in any gangs, as far as anyone reported. Thanks to my mother.

My mother was thrilled when I got my certificate in website development, and I passed a bunch of the industry's own exams, and I was hired for a job I wanted. At least one of her kids was making good. "I'm so so glad," she kept saying. Her only disappointment was that I didn't have to wear a jacket and tie to work—IT people were casual—but she was over the moon that I worked in a high-rise in Manhattan. Actually, I was too, in my jaded way. I liked that job, but I lost it in the Crash. I went through a bunch of jobs, those first years.

I moved out of my mother's, but I never moved out of Queens, which was how I heard about Veronica's husband. People told people. My friend, Binh, got the news from his sister, Veronica's friend since kindergarten. The husband had been killed crossing a street at night in Leeds,

England, hit by a speeding taxi when he came out of a pub and looked right instead of left.

"Shit," I said. "I can't believe it." It was the wrong story for this husband, someone that young, that protected. "Shit. Veronica wasn't hurt, right?"

"She was in New York. He was over there shooting some documentary about the history of fabric mills. You going to call her?"

"Of course, I'm going to call her," I said. "She's okay?"

"How could she be okay?" Binh said. "They were married five years. She's a widow."

"Hey, Joe," she said, softly. "Hi."

I made a botch of saying how sorry I was, but she was used to that by now. "Everybody's calling," she said.

"Tell me if there's anything I can do. Tell me if you need anything."

"I'm okay," she said. "I have everything. My mom comes every day and cooks for me, just so I don't fade away."

"You'll be okay," I said. "You were always strong."

"People keep saying that," she said. "I hate it."

"Sorry," I said.

"Except you," she said. "You can say it."

❖ ❖ ❖

And what was she going to do now? Everybody in the neighborhood was wondering. She hadn't worked at a job since her lunch shifts in the college cafeteria; the husband had supported her. Binh's sister said that the husband—his name was Schuyler, did I know that?—and his two brothers had all come into some part of the family holdings when they turned twenty-one. And whatever he had in his bank account was Veronica's, wasn't it?

Probably the money wasn't just in the bank either; it was invested in things, different things. Did the man have a will? Veronica (I made a point of phoning her now, checking in) was pretty sure he'd never gotten around to making one. A lawyer someone had told her to consult said it might take a year to sort everything out, but she was next of kin, and if there were no other claims (none yet), it should all go smoothly.

My ex-girlfriend was about to be an heiress. Talking about this directly (which plenty of people did) appalled her. "I get *congratulated*," she said. As if her future windfall was a payment for having lost Schuyler, a crass profit. As if she'd made a lucky deal. I reminded her how she'd once been a big fan of Dickens's *Great Expectations*—we had to read it in high school—and now she was like Pip, waiting for her big legacy to come in.

"But Pip gets tricked about the legacy part," she said. "He thinks his allowance is all from crazy rich Miss

Havisham. All that training to be a gentleman. He guesses totally wrong about where it's coming from."

"At least it comes," I said.

"People are very crude about wills in those nineteenth-century novels," she said. She'd been an English major in college, perfect preparation for not having a job. "All those family members with their claws out, waiting for some rich aunt to keel over. Their main chance."

"Nobody hates money," my American father always said. An undeniable fact, all over the world, but he had a way of saying it that sounded smug. *He* wasn't short on that wanted commodity. But nobody gets to have everything forever, and a few years after my mother fought with him about my brother Jack, he lost his health, pretty much, and he wasn't even that old. He had a stroke, and then he must've had more strokes, and from the last hospital stay he somehow talked my mother into bringing him home with her and taking care of him. He lay around in the living room watching TV and giving orders and slobbering over plates of her food. Helping him into the tub was a hideous production she used to sometimes enlist me in.

My mother tended him well, she never neglected him, and he was a pain in the ass. She took care of whatever he wanted for more than a year, before he died in his sleep on the couch in the living room.

Veronica told me that Schuyler, her husband, had always liked England, and he'd been having a good time on the film shoot. He had a cheerful level of alcohol in his bloodstream when he stepped out into that street—he loved the ale there—and traces of hash were in his system too. Hash, not marijuana? Veronica said she wasn't up on his recent hobbies. The two of them hadn't been talking all that much, in the six months before his death. That was news. They'd been in a detached phase, she said, an unfaithful phase, on both sides, and maybe they'd been on their way out as a couple. "I'll never know, will I?" she said. Now she was having one-way conversations with him across the great divide, still waiting for the worst not to be true. Now she had things to tell him.

And she had dreams. In one dream Schuyler kept saying they were late for a party, they had to rush to get there, but they couldn't get themselves out of the apartment. They kept remembering gas jets left burning, sinks filling with water, urgent phone calls they had to make. She knew it was a trivial dream to have, under the circumstances, but it had its own torment and dread. And the party was definitely going on without Schuyler; that part, she said, was right.

✦ ✦ ✦

So we had coffee one Sunday when she was out in Queens visiting her parents. I didn't know how I'd expected her to look, but she looked different. Her mouth was tighter and her eyes smaller; she hadn't lost her prettiness but it was a little distorted. She looked better when she greeted me, *Hey, you*, as if the sight of me amused her. We were in the coffee shop we used to go to, with its Formica tables and quilted vinyl booths.

She felt light as a bird when she got up to hug me. "It's kind of a bad day," she said, "but I'm so glad to see you." She had her hair long and straight, same as ever.

"This booth has missed you," I said. "It wants someone to spill ketchup on it."

"No one's as good at that as I am."

She could've looked me up before, I thought. Maybe not. She was married.

"I just got some not very good news," she said. "From my lawyer."

Schuyler's parents, who lived in Colorado, had decided to legally contest the distribution of his assets to Veronica. Copies of the papers they'd filed had arrived in her lawyer's office on Friday. His two brothers (Schuyler was the youngest) had signed supporting statements. "I thought they liked me," she said. "I can't believe it, I can't."

"Blood is thicker," I said.

"Schuyler's family always wanted more of a wedding than we ever wanted—I thought maybe they were just thinking we weren't really married. I *have* the certificate, if anyone wants to see it. That's not it. They don't care."

They were arguing against her on other grounds, it turned out. Citing the compromised nature of her union with Schuyler, her failure to carry out the expected obligations of a wife, and Schuyler's most recent views and intentions for his future.

"They can do that?" I said.

"People do everything. The court decides. That's what my lawyer said."

"Fuck," I said.

"I used to listen for hours to his father's stupid views on foreign policy. I used to let his overdressed mother tell me how to do my hair," she said. "Do they think I killed their son? What do they think?"

"It's not necessarily personal," I said.

"His brother Rick used to let me beat him at Ping-Pong; his brother Taddy loved my key lime pie. I thought we were fine."

"People like to keep cash in the family," I said. "Especially when there's a lot of it."

✦ ✦ ✦

"I can do without all the money," Veronica said, the next time we talked on the phone. "What did I ever do, that it should just fall into my lap like that?" An uncle of hers had passed out flyers for McGovern when he ran for president in 1972 and still said it was a shame the man never got to put through his graduated inheritance tax—100 percent for anyone left more than half a million. "I know. Who re-members George McGovern?" Veronica said. "Is he dead? I don't think he's dead."

"He's dead," I said.

"And I never objected for a second," she said, "to coming into Schuyler's money."

"People don't," I said.

What if I had married Veronica when she was so eager to get married? We might have been totally fine; we might've made a nest for our stupid young selves. Rushing into things could be extremely intelligent. By now we might've had a kid already. I could imagine all of it, was that odd? She probably could too. We could've done it without money.

"We're surrounded by TV shows and movies teaching useless crap," she said. "Everybody is raised to think the one way to get ahead is to want more and more."

Everybody meant Americans. Veronica was always the white American kid in a neighborhood getting more Asian every day. Some of her friendships were because of me. Binh and his sister Kim were Vietnamese, my brother and

I were half-Thai, her friend Suravi's family was Bengali.
Well, we all wanted money. Didn't we?

While she was ranting, I was thinking that only Buddhists were against wanting more. My mother, I had to say,
was not that kind of Buddhist. But she talked about the theory of not wanting, she did that much. She exposed me to it.

If I had married Veronica, we could have had a honeymoon in Montauk, right on the Atlantic. Not that far
away. She always liked the beach, and I could've gotten us a
room with an ocean view; I could've done that much.

Our friends had opinions about Schuyler's family. "What
a bunch of bloodsucking Ivy League vampire assholes,"
Binh's sister said.

"Those pathetic jerks," Suravi said. "They were too
shitty and cowardly and sneaky to even tell her before they
cut her out."

"Rich people are fucks," Binh said.

It took a long time, all of it. There were delays; there were
long expensive conversations between Veronica and her
lawyer (was he any good?). Her mother kept saying, "Honey,
I had no idea this could happen." The warring heirs, the
merciless acquisition of wealth by scheming and slander,

a family's insatiable avarice. Who could imagine all that? Miss Havisham? Abel Magwitch? Uncle Pumblechook?

The family's papers said that Schuyler had voiced intentions to end the marriage, that he planned to marry a young woman from Leeds, England (Maribel, what kind of name was that?), and that Veronica had been an unfit spouse. They cited two persons with whom she'd had brief affairs (a woman from her book group and a man who worked at a nearby bar). Okay, that part was true. Her past friends, they said, included a known criminal (this meant my brother Jack, who had a bullshit juvie arrest for drug possession), and she herself had failed to respond to phone calls when Schuyler was abroad, possibly owing to drug use; her husband had chosen to spend increasing amounts of time away due to his belief that she had falsely presented herself in their earliest acquaintance. Veronica's lawyer rested their sole defense very heavily on the incontrovertible fact that she and Schuyler had been, whatever the fuck anyone said, really married.

Veronica never wanted to say that her lawyer was no good, but theirs was probably wonderful. In the end, the surrogate court decided entirely in favor of Schuyler's parents. The money went to them, and they didn't even need it.

Veronica was never going to see them again either. She'd fantasized about showing great generosity of spirit if she won, forgiving them so beautifully they had to appreciate her again. But no one wanted to be fond of a person they'd just been successfully rotten to. That was the end of having any in-laws.

Or any free income. Of course, she could have a perfectly good life anyway. "Who put *them* in charge of my destiny?" she said. But it was going to take some scrambling she didn't know how to do, involve plans she didn't have yet. Why didn't she?

"I don't know how to do anything," she told me. "What did I go to college for if I don't know anything?" She wondered what Schuyler would tell her to do now. I thought she should get her employment counseling elsewhere, but I didn't say so. "I'm thinking about what that Maribel looks like," she said. "Probably very cool-looking, if she worked on the film with him."

I was losing some of my patience with Veronica. A janitor's daughter, no reason she couldn't just roll up her sleeves and get to it, start anywhere.

"She's acting stupid because she's depressed," Kim said.

My mother, who had once been horrified at Veronica the American turning me into a teenage husband, said, "When she has no food, she will find a job."

I'd never understood my mother's life. There were other men she liked, closer to her age, but she always let my father creep back. My brother and I were hardly ever glad to see him, despite his silly playing and his efforts to entertain us. Well, I liked him when I was very little. Jack went silent if he was around. He used to stomp on our father's coat in secret and then later he stole bills from his wallet and once a credit card. My mother said we were spoiled, we knew nothing. Spoiled by our father's money.

What money? All the years we were growing up, our mother worked long hours as hostess at the Golden Treasure Thai Restaurant (where I later washed dishes). Maybe they paid her so badly she had to keep getting his contributions. Which probably were not reliable.

In the days when Veronica and I were a high school couple, she did meet my father a few times. She noticed, as everyone did, that I looked like him. I had the chin; I had my own version of the nose, which threw people off about what I was. She thought his fake-youthful dyed hair was a hoot—she wrapped a black T-shirt around her head to imitate him to me. We made fun of everyone then. My father's hair grew out when he was sick, went all the way to white. He was looking startled and ghostly at the end.

But I missed him after he was gone. *Missed* might not be the right word—I didn't want his company, but I wanted his presence in the world. I was sorry for myself when he died.

✦ ✦ ✦

My mother was from Isan, the poorest part of Thailand, in the Northeast. She and her sister had come to Bangkok as young girls to work as maids in a big hotel where a cousin had found them jobs. It was there she met my father, and she got pregnant with me two years into their romance. Her sister married a construction worker in the city and went on to have three kids with him. From New York my mother used to send them money when she could; years later she sent them my brother, not much of a gift.

How did my brother get by over there in Bangkok? He said that speaking two languages was a big asset in a city full of tourists. Different scams, that meant. He remembered Veronica perfectly well; he always liked her. "Bring her over here," he said. "It'll cheer her up."

"I'm not doing any bringing," I said.

My mother didn't talk all that much about her childhood, except sometimes. Her father was a rice farmer—a tenant farmer, never a good thing to be. Even in okay years, the kids were sent out to catch lizards and bugs; her grandmother trapped moths with a candle and served them on rice. They ate rats too—my mother said they were tasty—but only field rats; nobody ate house rats.

"Nothing special, everyone else the same," she said, if we shrieked at any of it. How good my father must have looked to her, with money pouring out of his pockets. I guess we always knew that. My brother had his own version of my mother's stories. *My mama so poor the ducks threw bread at her.*

We didn't grow up rich by American standards, since my father wasn't around all that much. We never saw any doctors or dentists, not then, and I was supposed to be Jack's babysitter, a job I hated and did not excel at. We had food from the restaurant, we did have that, and we had a TV, which helped my mother learn English.

Binh's sister Kim called me to talk about Veronica. "She won't go out of the apartment, she's living on nothing but cold cereal, and I think she's getting evicted soon."

"She has parents," I said.

"She doesn't want them to know. They already paid for the lawyer when all the husband's funds got frozen. Took a big bite out of savings they don't have."

"She has to get a job, she knows that," I said.

"When I call, I can't get a word out of her. She's not good."

She'd talk to me, I thought, and I phoned Veronica right away. "Hey, girl," I said. "What's up?"

"I was just taking a nap," she said. "I have to rest for my job interview."

"What's it for?"

"Receptionist at a magazine publisher. I have to learn to use the phone system though."

"You'll do great."

"They hated me at my other interview."

"Part of the process." I was full of wisdom, wasn't I?

"Got to hang up," she said. "I always eat a bowl of Special K before I go to an interview."

"Protein is good."

"And I'm washing my hair."

It turned out the interview was for the next day. She had to wash a certain shirt too—did I think it could dry in time?

I was thinking, even if they hired her they wouldn't pay her for a month, if she lasted that long. "I can lend you some bucks to tide you over till you get on your feet," I said.

I had no idea I was going to say that, and it was too late to take it back.

"You don't have to," she said.

"It just happens to be something I want to do," I said. I was showing off. "Humor me."

I said this as many ways as I could. It would save me lots of worry just to know she was okay, we'd known each other since fourth grade, friends could make loans to other friends, what were friends for. I argued so well I persuaded myself, and how much convincing did she need? Probably not this much.

"I'm so lucky I know you," she said. She took the money, a couple thousand.

✦ ✦ ✦

Binh said, "Does the phrase *fucking idiot* mean anything to you?"

Some friends thought the loan was a kind of special payment, for sex or whatever, an unspoken bargain we had struck. Who wanted to buy sex? I hadn't lacked for girlfriends all these years and was currently dating someone I liked fine (I wasn't telling her about this loan either).

I did wonder if people leaped to conclusions about me because of my mother. Maybe they assumed that I was used to a cynical view of love and money. All of this made me especially careful not to come on to Veronica. Which was not to say I didn't think of her that way. We had our own private history of discovery and bodily amazement, of inventing our own brilliant systems. It wasn't a neutral memory.

But I kept away from her after I sent her a check in the mail. I started to pay more attention to Lily, the woman I'd been seeing for a while. She got me running with her on weekends, a pastime I'd resisted (what was wrong with staying still?) until I fell into the habit of it. On clear fall weekends, we ran through the streets, making up our own routes. It bonded us, even though we didn't speak as we did it. At the end, we'd park our overheated selves under a tree, drink fortified water, and lean against each other. How pretty Lily looked then, her skin flushed, her hair tied back.

◆ ◆ ◆

And Veronica wasn't phoning me. She lost the apartment anyway, it turned out, and she moved in with Kim (who already had a roommate), and she slept on Kim's sofa, not the worst thing.

"I told you," Binh said. "Don't hold your breath about that loan."

"I don't care," I said.

"What are you, made of money?"

"I like to think I'm made of something else," I said, and no wonder he snorted. You could never say money didn't come first; no one would believe you. But I wasn't lying.

"You don't think she's using you?" Binh said, an odd thing to utter about someone like Veronica. Didn't we all think she was clueless and innocent? Kept young and childish by not working?

"No one's more selfish than a kid," Binh said. "Remember us."

"I don't care," I said. "I'm fine. It's like what they say about the stock market: never invest more than you can afford to lose."

"Said like a billionaire," Binh said.

Of course, I was not prepared for the catastrophe with my brother. My mother got a phone call from her sister in Bangkok with the news that he'd run into some trouble with the police. He'd been giving two tourist girls directions, sitting over their maps with them at a café, and one of them discovered too soon that her passport was gone. He probably wasn't good at it; he always overrated himself. The girl yelled, the café owner went after him as he was leaving, Jack punched the guy, it was a mess. The police now had to be given a substantial monetary tribute to show honor and respect.

We wired the money to my mother's sister; someone in the family could go deal with this. My aunt didn't want to send either of her daughters, and her son was currently down with a round of dengue fever. People got that in Bangkok? My uncle was out of town on a job. Meanwhile my brother, Jack, was stuck in jail. "There's no time!" my mother said. "No waiting! Not good!" I had to go, I knew that.

Lily, my girlfriend, was horrified, not that it was really any of her affair. She thought I was getting sucked into a bad business, and I should just say no, why didn't I? The accusation of weakness especially infuriated me—she had no clue—and I said some things to her I could never unsay.

I did call Veronica the night before I left. I had to leave a message—"Don't worry if you can't reach me, family matters call me to the home country." I hadn't been to Thailand since I was a fetus in utero. It certainly wasn't home, but my first day there was like an overheated, unearthly dream of home, filled with fast-talking relatives and half-familiar faces. My aunt kept screeching with delight at the sight of me, very unlike the way my mother acted. Not that I minded delighting anyone. The daughters and their husbands yammered at me in a Thai I couldn't always follow.

It was a day before I could get in to see my brother, and he was not a pretty sight, pimpled and skinny and a little smelly, wearing the brown shorts and T-shirt of the jail uniform. "Hey, bro," he said, "welcome to Asia, what took you so long?" I laughed just to hear him. He was still Jack.

We were in a back room of the police station, separated by bars. I would've known him anywhere, but he wasn't a teenager anymore. "You look very good, maybe too good," he said to me. What I should do was this: talk to the fat cop not the tall one, never offer anything directly, flatter their lovely system, slip the guy more than *that*. He was glad they hadn't sent our lame-ass cousin to manage this. "This isn't some party here, you know." It was all very harrowing. A cop came to cuff my brother and walk him downstairs to the cells.

I hated Jack when I went back to my aunt's. In Thailand it was a crime, same as anywhere, to offer a bribe—did anyone worry about me? Jack could manage better in jail or prison than I could. Everyone thought I was so smart, but I didn't know what I was doing.

Fear made me go very slowly. I visited whenever they let me, I spoke politely to any police I was near, I brought them cigarettes and fruit. I tried to talk about soccer matches (that went nowhere). I saw my chance when one cop lingered with me, as I was being led to the door. I had so much fear in me I hardly made sense when I mentioned how grateful we were to everyone there, how highly we thought of them, how hard we knew they all worked, and he took the envelope with our wishes.

My brother got out a day later, charges dismissed. My aunt cooked a big rowdy dinner to celebrate, and Jack kept handing me bottles of beer and saying, "You did it, bro." We facetimed our mother from my phone, panning a long shot of all the revelers, and I was quite delirious myself. What a great, goofy family I had. Very late that night Jack went back to wherever he lived—on a canal, he said, but I never saw it. "Love to everyone," he said on my voicemail the next day. "Love to Mom, thank everyone." And I couldn't get him on the phone after that. For a day I left messages and texts, and the next day a recorded voice in Thai said the number was out of service.

So I flew home, job done, back to my work, back to my perfectly good life. I went at once to my mother, bringing her a smuggled jar of bamboo-shoot soup from Aunt Tukta. "Very proud," she said, meaning of me and what I had done in the police station. She was upset, of course, that Jack had slipped away from all of us. Not for the first time. "We'll hear," I said. "When he wants." But her real disappointment, it turned out, was that I had failed to bring my brother back with me. That was her plan? I was supposed to buy him a ticket? "You have charge card," she said.

When my brother first left, when he was still a sixteen-year-old wiseass, my mother wept at the airport. We weren't at all used to her that way. My embarrassed brother said, "You sound like a pigeon or something," and she made a miserable attempt at chuckling. She said, through her tears, "They will like you in Bangkok," a city she hadn't seen since before he was born. Her visa had long since run out, and she was afraid that if she went home she could never come back. She should've found an American to marry, but she didn't.

I told everybody back at work what a great time I'd had in Thailand. My relatives fed me amazing food nonstop and of course took me all over so I saw everything, it wasn't that pretty a city except for the temples but it was on a river and the canals were great. "Bet you partied hearty," people said. There was a backlog of work waiting for me, tangles of data to be strung and ordered, and I couldn't understand how I had ever done any of it. I stayed late, looking at the same material over and over. What did this data ever mean? I was scaring myself by my denseness.

I had a month at work that was so bad that when I asked to take a leave, my supervisor said he would have to think about whether my eventual return was feasible. I went home in a rage against the longstanding outrageous use of me by tech-industry assholes, by my crazy mother and my fucked-up family and my criminal brother who were happy to soak me for whatever I had, by every spoiled princess of a woman I'd ever been with.

I shouldn't have called Veronica that night but I did. She answered right away, too, on her cell, wherever she was.

"I'm inviting you over," I said. "Now, I mean. Come visit."

"It's kind of late," she said. It was around ten.

"No, it isn't."

"I get up early to bake now. I work for my friend, Cindy, you don't know her, she designs cakes for people. I work for her, I like it."

"You at Kim's still?"

"No, I'm subletting in Astoria."

"You can come over," I said. "Astoria. Don't tell me you can't. I don't want to hear it. You owe me that much."

And she stopped trying to tell me. When she turned up forty-five minutes later, I hugged her at the door. She was dressed more downscale than ever, in a sweatshirt, and

she hadn't put on any makeup for me. "Looking great," I
told her.

"I never saw your house, this is your house?" she said.
I lived in a big studio apartment, littered with magazines
and running clothes at the moment. I wondered if she'd
thought I was doing better than this.

I poured her a glass of Mekhong whiskey with a lot of
ice; I brought out some very decent cheese from the fridge. I
asked her about the cakes she made; I wasn't rude. "They're
so beautiful," she said. "Some people do these bright, car-
toony cakes, but ours are more floral and sculpted." It was
true she'd always liked to cook. Once when we were in high
school, she made me a truffled mac 'n' cheese, really good,
which I now reminded her of.

For all the sappiness of this conversation, she knew why
I'd asked her over. While we were standing in the kitchen
getting more ice, she laughed in recognition when I made
my move, when I reached for her. She wasn't eager the way
she'd once been, I could tell that right away, but she stayed
with whatever we were doing.

It was my call. I had her pressed against the kitchen
wall; I had both of us wrapped in a monster's appetite. A
friendly monster, I meant her no harm, but when I got us
to the sofa, when the clothes came off and we started in
earnest, what we were doing was fucking. It wasn't anything sweeter. Most of it felt great—I was glad, in a defiant

way—it took me where I wanted to go, gave me something of what I was owed.

Afterward I was close to contented, stilled and spent and proud that I'd had this idea. I wasn't a helpless half-wit, I'd had the sense to know what I could call on, what reserves I had. "Hey, girl," I said. There was Veronica, with her hair across her face, crumpled and rosy and mashed into the couch. I moved to give her room.

"I have to go," she said, "it's late."

"You want tea? I can make you tea."

"No, thanks."

"More whiskey?"

"Not now."

"Thank you for the great reunion."

"Anytime," she said. "But it's late."

"It's not that late," I said, and I held her in a solid grip. I didn't want to let her go that fast—she could remember her reasons to be thankful to me, if she wanted to. "What's the big rush?" She didn't answer, and she lay very still inside my clasping arm. Let her think she was my prisoner; I didn't care just then. She could wait a minute. "Sleep," I said.

I worked on keeping us motionless and I was even starting to drift off, when she said, "I really have to go."

"I know." I took my arm away; I sat up. She was off of that couch before I knew it. "I'll call you a cab. I don't want you wandering around at this hour."

I watched her dress while I tapped the Uber app on my phone. Had her body changed since we'd been high school sweethearts? Not much, not at all. The lush bareness was disappearing under her clothes now (she was always a fast dresser). "All ready," she said.

I walked her downstairs, and I had my arm around her while we waited for the car. "I have to get up at five," she said. "We're doing somebody's anniversary party."

"You're very dedicated," I said.

"I am," she said.

"But you came over anyway."

"Well."

When I helped her into the car, she turned away before I got in much of a kiss. "Nice to see you," she said. She didn't bother sounding sincere but why should she? She was sturdier than people thought; she was going to be all right. And she still had my two thousand bucks.

My mother was horrified that I was out of work. "They fired you?" I explained that my status wasn't settled, maybe I could go back, maybe not. "You must find new job," she suggested.

This was not the worst idea. My father liked to talk about new brooms sweeping clean. He was full of self-assured platitudes, and some of them were right. My mother still kept a photo of him on a shelf, an old one with a head of dark hair, with a vase next to it that usually held a fresh flower. Did she really think any efforts on her part (she gave alms to the local temple in his name) could get him reborn into a better realm?

One of the big questions of my father's life had been "What can money buy?" It bought my mother's company; that was the initial lure. He believed in money, he wanted everything bound to him by it, as if it were surer than other ties. A dark theory, and my brother and I were the proof it didn't work with kids. My brother used to make a point of destroying most of the gifts he gave us, but of course that was my brother.

Now Jack was over there palming tourists' passports. We weren't a family above money, were we? Look at how I had behaved with Veronica, calling in my debt. She'd understood me perfectly well, as I'd known she would. Well, nobody forced her. I kept remembering her getting into the car, turning her head away. That night wasn't ever going to turn into just nothing. Had I thought it would? Had I thought at all?

"Good news," my mother said. "Jack is good." My brother had phoned her, late the night before, when she'd just gotten back from the restaurant. "Sounding good," she told me. He was sorry for being out of touch, he'd gotten busy with tasks that required his attention outside of Bangkok. He was extremely grateful to my mother for helping him and also to me. And now he was fine, working in a friend's store, selling phones, everybody needed a phone, and phone cards.

"He can call for cheap now," I said.

"Yes," she said. "This is nice. And he's earning very well from those phones. His friend likes him."

"Maybe he'll be the rich one," I said. "Richer than me." My efforts at reemployment were not a raging success.

Later in the week, around midnight, I too had a phone call from Jack. "Hey, my ace," he said. "I never thanked you."

"You did," I said. "And everybody toasted me many times over at Aunt Tukta's. I got completely hammered on beer and that rice booze. You okay now?"

"Doing well," he said. "New work, new girl I'm living with. You saw me at a low point. I hope you didn't tell Mom how bad I looked."

"No need."

"I look much cuter now," he said. "Believe me."

I was out of work a lot longer than I expected. Whatever they wanted, they didn't seem to think I had it, and I wasn't getting a rave from my last employer. I found myself eating Cheerios for supper one night, while I watched the news on my computer. Only someone like Veronica could survive on cereal for weeks. After dinner I read the *Times* online, all of it. In the Food section, in the pieces on hip new things to eat, there was a photo of two women standing behind a cake iced in the shape of a giant peony, and one of the women was Veronica, with her hair pulled back. It really was, the caption said so. "Sweet Blooms for Easter Table" was the heading, with the report that guests would swoon over the pandan-flavored lily and the black-sesame violets as well. A noted rock star was already a fan.

Fuck, I thought, *everybody's doing well but me.* I made efforts to conquer the pettiness of this point of view. Apparently Veronica was getting up in the morning for an actual purpose and her dedication was paying off. And they were pictured as co-bakers, so maybe she had been promoted too. I left her a text: *Saw thing in paper bravo to u bake on girl.*

My mother had seen the thing too. "Apron not flattering," she said. She wanted me to settle down, but not with Veronica.

"The cakes are great," I said. I had a fantasy that if I ever had a wedding, I'd buy a big expensive fantastic floral cake from Veronica, to show that my feelings were larger than my mistakes and my loyalty was unswerving. I got quite carried away with the idea and how the cake would look.

Meanwhile I could barely buy a bag of potato chips. At the end of one very dispiriting week—could people at least reply to say I wasn't their type?—I was summoned for an interview. The manager who talked to me was a highly pretty woman, Mei Something—fabulous short haircut— who liked me, I could tell, and our interview lasted longer than some. At the end she told me how much she loved Thai food, people always said that, and I had to chuckle and admit what a good cook I was (total lie). A week went by without a word and another week. Maybe I'd flirted too much. But I hadn't really.

One night I was hanging out with Binh, watching some ridiculous boys-on-a-bender comedy on his TV, and I checked for email on my phone. No one had written about hiring me, but there was a weird message from PayPal.

"Watch out for scams," Binh said. "Do *not* give them any info."

Money had allegedly been sent to me from a PayPal account under the name L. Lots, by email from Lotsofbetter. And the amount was odd—it was $856.18. I tried to decode those numbers—Veronica's birthday was in August, the eighth month, but I couldn't get her day and year to fit with the other numbers. She was a person who could be superstitious, could invent little rituals. What percentage of $2,000 was $856.18? The numbers meant nothing that I could decode, except that she wanted to start paying back and was making a prank out of it, to get away from the heavy-handed exchange of cash.

I explained this to Binh, who said, "You really want to click anything on that site?"

The site checked out as actually being PayPal—I could get under the layers that much, geek that I was—and it was asking me to click to send the funds to my checking account that they already knew. What the fuck. I did it.

I went to bed sure that everything financial with my name on it was now crashing in the dark. Not that I had enough to care. I woke up very early and saw the bank app on my phone had deposit news, and I'd no sooner run out the door than, right on my own corner, real bills came out of the cash machine. I emailed Lotsofbetter—*Very charming surprise. Spending it wisely.*

What is it with luck? No sooner was I wolfing down an extravagant breakfast—delicious eggs Benedict at a café I had to walk twenty minutes to—than I found a message from the lovely Mei, asking if I could come in again for a second interview. I could indeed.

And that was the beginning of the new phase in my life. They hired me, the job was fine, I pulled myself together, I showed up early and worked hard. And I refrained from coming on to Mei inappropriately—did I need to get either of us fired? I did not. We had a lot of chats in the coffee room, and I kept things harmless.

Veronica and the cleverness of her repayment were still on my mind. Apparently she was going for installments, as her finances slowly got ahead. But I never got her on the phone again, no matter when I called or what I said in the message. No replies from texts or the usual email either. She was more responsive on Lotsofbetter (maybe she only used that account now)—I did hear *Congrats great news*, when I sent word about the job. *Congrats*, who said that? She didn't want us to be a couple—I got it—and she was right.

And just when I never expected it, I got another surprise message from PayPal. This one was for $980.85. Hadn't we first met each other in September, the ninth month? Was the first day of school September 8? But the 085 didn't signify anything. I was being too literal about these numbers; she had a more encrypted system.

I sent my thanks to Lotsofbetter—*Well done. I like being amazed by cash falling from the sky.*

So now she was choosing to talk to me only through money. Money, of course, was always said to talk, which meant that it had a very loud voice and could drown out all else. I began to wonder if I should give all the money back to her. By now I'd been working at the job for six months, and these little payments from cyberspace weren't needed to rescue me. What if the weird sum of these two odd amounts suddenly appeared in her account? What if I just brushed away her filthy shekels? Oh, we'd be going in circles. Back to you, back to *you*. It wouldn't be a real answer to the chilliness of her not speaking to me.

I was brooding over this at one in the morning, when the phone rang with Jack calling me from Thailand. *This can't be good news*, I thought, but it was. "Doing great," he said. "June wants to see New York. I got us tickets." June was the new girlfriend (lots of Bangkok women liked English names). "Coming in ten days. You think you can stand it?"

"Mom will be ecstatic. In fact, tell her it was my idea."

"I want to take us all out for dinner, so think of a good spot. I'm okay now for cash. Well, you know that, from the PayPal stuff I sent. I never forget that you bailed me out. I don't forget."

I had the self-control not to bellow out loud. My brother had fooled me, he'd let me think it was all Veronica. How insane my messages must have sounded to her. I knew full well that I alone had managed to trick myself, but it was hard to stop being furious at Jack.

"Joe?" he said to me. "You there?"

"I'll find us a great place," I said. "What kind of food does June like?"

"Everything. I knew I could put you on it," he said. "Be great to see you."

"I'll tell Mom not to be mean to the woman."

Veronica must have thought I was mocking and goading her, constantly sending sarcastic messages about a debt she hadn't paid. I was never getting any of that money back now. Of course, I didn't need to, because my brother had sent me quite a bit of it. Those ragged figures must have been Thai baht converted to dollars. Why didn't I think of that? And he never wanted to use his name for anything, never.

My brother had behaved very handsomely, for him. He'd done his best to gather up his hard-earned black-market profits and rain golden coins on me. The envelope of bills I gave to the Thai cops for him had actually come from our mother, with a final addition from me on-site, but I'd paid my own absurdly overpriced last-minute airfare.

When we were kids, I had to take him with me if our mother was at work. I'd make fun of him to my friends, I'd stop him when he talked, I'd give him rope burns with my hands. I hadn't been very fair to him but brothers aren't. He was a tough bird, even as a little kid.

When he got older, he stole candy, usually Snickers, my

favorite, which he turned over to me. He'd cross the street in traffic, dashing around cars, and never get killed. He was always trying to impress me.

And when he was only fifteen, the police, trying to get more active in the neighborhood, stopped and frisked him (Bloomberg was mayor) and found a joint in his pocket. Not necessarily a big deal, but they drove him to the station to scare him. My mother was afraid to appear in such a place, unregistered alien that she was, and I was almost eighteen by then, so I was the one to fetch him. He waited till we were out on the street to sound like Jack. "They have the IQs of cockroaches, those cops," he said.

"Your job right now is to shut up," I said. "Around Mom particularly. Don't go on about any cops. You okay? How bad was it?" That was the best I did for him; I should've done more.

Now my mother was beside herself with joy that he was coming back from Thailand to see us. She wanted to decorate the living room with crepe paper streamers, and should she get a new dress? Everything she had was too old. "I can't believe it," she said, beaming, and I saw how afraid she'd been of his never showing up again.

"He likes this girlfriend," I said. "We have to be very nice to her. Try your best, Mom."

She laughed, in her high spirits. "Very, very nice," she said.

She wanted to have a big feast for him, with all his favorite foods from Golden Treasure Thai.

"I think he wants to take us out for the first dinner," I said. "He wants to treat us royally."

"Afterward we come here for dessert," she said. "Big celebration here after. Wine, beer, whiskey, big dessert."

I knew where we could get a terrific dessert. I could order, like anyone else, from the Perfect Flower Cake Bakery, where Veronica and her friend Cindy sculpted their buttercream marvels. I'd sign up online—with my real name, nothing to hide—and I'd go pick it up in person, who would stop me? Plenty of time to order. And which flower did my mother think people would like?

It was Mei, in our coffee-room chats, who told me about the bankruptcy; she was much more up on business news than I was. The famous department stores founded by Veronica's husband's family were going under, filing for bankruptcy while their debtors clamored. I shocked Mei by guffawing at this news. "Too complicated to explain," I said. I sort of hoped Veronica was crowing at the downfall too. Maybe the inheritance from Schuyler would just have come to nothing anyway, only a lot of bum stock. Money like dried leaves blowing away in the proverbial wind.

The bankruptcy was in billions and was taking down some suppliers. Once I heard the story, I looked everything up online. There were the brothers, Tad and Richard, two thirtyish guys in suits walking up the steps of a courthouse. Punished for their bad behavior to Veronica.

Two brothers. One article said rumors had them quarreling with each other, vying for different strategies. Alternate forms of legal skullduggery. *Stick together*, I could have told them. *Don't make it worse.*

I went to pick up the cake on my lunch hour, out to Brooklyn, hunting down some side street in Crown Heights, ignoring the option of delivery. The bakery was a tiny storefront with nothing but a majestic pile of sculpted orchids in the window, some pale, some brilliant, braced against the log that was my cake. "It looks fantastic," I said, coming through the door. Behind the counter was Veronica, with her hair in a kerchief.

"It does," she said. "Hi, Joe."

"Hello, hello. Hey, I heard about the bankruptcy," I said. "What a thing."

"You know why they went under?" she said. "They were greedy in a stupid way. Only paid themselves." She was getting out a flat white cardboard and folding it into a box. "Sometimes I think Schuyler was like them. He didn't have

75

to leave me with nothing. I cooked for him all those years; I took care of the apartment. But they picked on him too, you know, they were mean to him."

"The bakery smells fabulous."

"It does," she said. "Very good atmosphere for working yourself to the bone. I love it."

"The cake is for my brother—he's back all of a sudden for a visit. My mom is over the moon."

"Little naughty Jack. What's he like now?"

"He's good," I said. "He's been sending me money and I didn't even realize it, the way he did it. I think he's fine. Sorry for the emails with the crazy thanks."

She gave me a long stare. "I don't make very much. Even if we're doing well. I don't know what you think."

She was never going to like me again. Why should she? I was thinking of her face that night when she turned away. "I can't wait to try the cake," I said. And then I decided we had to shake hands. She seemed okay with that; we shook for a few seconds. We were done.

On the way home to Queens with the cake, I thought about how all religions hated money. Didn't they? Buddhist monks were supposed to own nothing but their begging bowls and clothes, Jesus threw the moneychangers out of the temple, Orthodox Jews couldn't carry cash on the

Sabbath. I was mad at money for the dirt it threw on my life. I never should have lent Veronica anything. Oh, was that the problem? I'd meant well, but not well enough. I behaved quite poorly, once I was poor. When I passed a bank near the subway station, I suddenly knew why people always wanted to bomb banks.

Not that I was planning to burn the contents of my wallet. It wasn't the bills' fault, no point blaming them; it was (as we liked to say) operator error. But still the bank looked creepy to me, with its columns like a Greek shrine and its vending machine open twenty-four hours.

The orchid cake could not have been a bigger hit. When my brother saw it, he yelled, "Oh, my God. What is that?"

"Special for you," my mother said. His girlfriend applauded, and then we all clapped too. For the cake.

We had just had our big meal out, at a terrific restaurant I picked for him in Brooklyn, in Dumbo. He had been a little hyper all evening, but in a good way. He told stories about nutty customers at the phone store and about the time Aunt Tukta set fire to the rice cooker. His girlfriend, whose English was not great, added extras to his stories in Thai, until we all switched. She wasn't what I expected—not that glamorous, a little chubby—but quite charmingly acerbic. She won me over. Even my mother snickered at her quips.

We had gone to meet them at the airport very late the night before. We hovered around the luggage area, and my brother saw us before we saw them. He ran straight for my mother and hugged her hard, like an American, right in public, while the girl looked confused and smiled. When I shook her hand and welcomed her to New York, she said in Thai, "Hello, brother who looks like Jack."

Jack said, "But I'm the better-looking one."

"No contest," my mother said. "Both perfect."

And on this evening of their first day, everyone was still pretty happy. We all said what a shame it was to cut a cake that looked like that, so we waited and got drunker. The traveling couple had napped all day—bad for jet lag; they'd be up for hours. "Whoever can stand on their head," Jack said, "has to cut the cake." This made no sense, but Jack did a headstand, with June holding his feet. "Cheating," I said. And then our mother did a headstand! I'd never seen such a thing. She fell over fast, legs landing on the sofa, but it was a new and great moment in our family. She got up, disheveled and giggling. Who was she?

The cake tasted fabulous, once the cuts were made. It had purple yam and coconut milk and maybe almond, was that almond? "You eat like this all the time?" June said.

Jack said, "I told her we grew up on leftovers. Now she'll never believe me."

"I never have," she said. He pretended to smack her on the arm and she smacked him back.

At some point in all the eating, June spotted the photo of my father, with a marigold in a vase next to it. "That's the sperm donor," I said. I said it in English, since I could only say it in Thai obscenely.

"My brother got along with him better than I did," Jack said. "And looks more like him too, don't you think?" Neither of us were the spitting image.

My mother said, "We remember him. You can see that we do."

The next day, I brought in a piece of cake to Mei. She saved it for a midmorning snack, and I watched her breaking off a bite-size chunk. "I'm not that into coconut," she said. "But it's incredibly thoughtful of you to bring it to me."

I heard in this bit of gratitude something that led me to suggest (out of earshot of anyone) an after-work drink together at a place two blocks away. I waited for her there, and in all our usual chitchat there was a thrum of lust you could've heard several miles away. We stayed a good two hours in the café, and then with no debate whatsoever we took a cab to her apartment and fell into bed at once, and that was the beginning of our secret coupleship, which was extremely sexy for being so against company policy and so long repressed and which should've happened a lot earlier.

After Jack went back to Bangkok with June, I tried not to neglect my mother, and so I told her about Mei a little sooner than I meant to. She announced that she was very pleased that both of us were settled, Jack and I. I didn't know how settled we were. Anyone could see we were destined for more upheavals. "About time," she said anyway, and I remembered that she'd been years younger than either of us when she first met our father. A girl of twenty from the village.

"So when you first met Dad," I said, "did you think it was going to last?"

"I didn't think anything," she said (she didn't want to answer).

The woman was still giving money to the monks for blessings on his behalf. What kind of religion did she have, bribing the cycle of karma with petty cash? And the flower she put every day in the vase by his picture: daily proof of how much I didn't know.

I could never guess if she got pregnant with me as a trick or by accident. My mother wasn't a schemer, but she grew up knowing how to bargain. Even in Queens she argued with anyone selling fruit on the street, and she always got the price down.

"Nobody *else* does that," Veronica used to say, "that haggling," and that was when she hoped to marry me too.

"Nothing wrong with it," I would say, very annoyed at Veronica.

And now my mother wanted to remind me that she made offerings quite often at the temple with special requests for Jack and me. My mother believed in deals, in concrete exchanges, in love or in anything. She thought I knew very little—about honor and price, the way of it. She always had to explain the obvious.

"I want you happy always with nice girls," she said. "Is that too much to ask?"

This was how she imagined our happiness? I thought of her long years with my father, the bargain she had made and mostly stuck to, though its original source was almost surely not love. How young she had been, when she made her first peace with her situation, made a settlement in her mind. She always told us how lucky we were, every day she said it, and it fell on deaf ears, for how could we know that then? Well-fed boy ingrates that we were. How could we know our luck?

3 / Maribel

THE LAST TIME I WAS IN LONDON, I KEPT PASSING store windows full of tea towels and souvenir mugs with the now-famous motto *Keep Calm and Carry On*. I read once that when the government dreamed up the slogan at the onset of World War II, the populace was insulted at being given advice that went without saying. Who wanted to Panic Badly and Fall Apart? Who needed to be instructed not to?

In Leeds, my home city, hardly anyone was buying such items (too few tourists), but in the all-too-brief spell in my life when I loved an American, he used to tease me by saying the words in my ear, if he thought I was worrying too much.

And what did I worry about then? I had no real problems.

His name was Schuyler, my American, and I met him on a film shoot where I was one of the runners. It was a documentary about textile mills in the nineteenth century, and I did minor tasks, getting everybody on the transit vans to the sites and making sure the lunch truck showed up. Schuyler, who was on the camera crew, never complained and was always decent to everyone. I knew he was going back to New York; I could see he had a wedding band. But I started it. We were all in a pub after work one night, a whole bunch of us, and I cornered him with questions. "Do you find Brits too pessimistic and resigned?" I said. "Do you think that's why we haven't been a world power for a while? Not that we should be."

Okay, it was an odd way of flirting, while everyone else was goofing around and telling fart jokes. "You don't seem pessimistic," he said. "I think you dress very cheerfully."

I was wearing a little summer dress that showed a lot of cleavage. "Thank you," I said. Was sex the hopeful side of my personality? I was interested in this insight, and my spirits were already starting to lift in his company.

He liked me too. It wasn't hard to get him to take me back to his hotel room. I had my own place but my flatmate Emilia could be a real pain. How outstanding Schuyler was, when I got to know him that way in his room, how sly and playful and endearing.

The hotel was a big clumsy modern place where everyone on the shoot was staying. I slipped out very early in the morning like a groupie—the man was married—but then the next night he told me not to go. Everyone knew anyway. Who cared? There was a nice buffet breakfast in the hotel, with sausages and bacon and eggs and grilled tomatoes and mushrooms. Bowls of melon balls.

What a glow the romance cast over my daily labors. I liked everything; no errand was too tedious. Sweep the front yard of a deserted mill? Find the next day's call sheets that some idiot lost? Tell the caterer one more time how many vegans we had? No problem. I was a model of sunny good nature, a production assistant sprinkled with pixie dust, and everybody did what I said. Everybody loved me.

The filming was going to take another four weeks, and my theory was that we had what we had. My whole life was still ahead of me, and I didn't think of myself as delicate. But why had he gotten married right out of college? Who did that anymore? I knew better than to ask, but I wanted to think he had felt sorry for her.

There was a rumor (a shoot was always full of rumors) that his family had buckets of money. This was irrelevant to me—I mostly paid for my own beers—and it was hard for us to tell about Americans from how they sounded. I myself didn't sound Northern, for instance, like some of the others in the crew, but Schuyler had no way to notice that.

"They own half the stores in the U.S.," my friend, Alastair, one of the other runners, told me. "I guess you're not going to get any fortune out of him though."

What I got out of him was the secret joy of our nights, which involved a lot of talking as well as casting off into further carnal waters. The talking was about family (if his parents always spoke about divorcing and never did, would they ever? would my father ever get over being a wreck?) and also about travel. My father used to work for companies in Bahrain and Abu Dhabi and I did secondary school in Qatar, a place most people can't even say right. I still had friends in Doha, Qatar's big city, and I thought I might really go live in Cairo sometime. I thought a lot of things. My mother lived in Leeds now, where she'd grown up, and my father was in London.

"Someday you'll come to New York," Schuyler said. We were lying in bed, half watching the TV when he said this, and I was thrilled to pieces—as if he were inviting me really—and I didn't say, *What'll you do with your wife?* I said, "I've never been to New York."

"Never? How could you hang out in Dubai and Amman and never visit the Big Apple?"

"I managed."

And this led to a running account of what I had to see in New York. The best bar in Brooklyn, which was in his neighborhood. The bike route up the west side of Manhattan to the George Washington Bridge. The best Korean taco truck. And of course the mummies at the Met and its Temple of Dendur, brought block by block from the Nile. The Chrysler Building had elevators that were Egyptian Art Deco—did I know that?

He didn't say all of this at once; he kept adding to the list whenever he saw me. "The ceiling with constellations at Grand Central Station," he'd say, when we passed each other on the set. "The pastrami sandwiches at Katz's." It was our joke—or his joke really, I just nodded—but it became something like a plan. How could I keep hearing about these things and not expect to see them?

Four weeks were longer than I'd thought, what with our being together every day. We had to get up at six a.m., which neither of us was good at—I was always cursing nonstop because I couldn't find a shoe, and Schuyler would emerge from the shower to remind me to keep calm and carry on. Such were our habits. One afternoon in the last week, we were filming at a complex of flax mills—zooming in on details of the Temple Works, an industrial building made to look like, of all things, an Egyptian temple. It was used for offices now. Nigel, our professorial expert on labor history in Yorkshire, was standing in front of this handsome structure talking about how children, hired to crawl under machines to pick up scraps, lost arms and legs to the machinery, and others were crippled from sixteen-hour days of cramped repeated motion. Overseers beat children with a strap when they didn't work well enough to keep up the pace. Nigel read a report of a child stripped and beaten unconscious. He had been intoning lines like this from the first, and we all talked about how outsourcing now was probably no better, but the man beating a child in rage over production levels brought me to tears. Schuyler also had wet eyes, I saw afterward. "Makes you ashamed of being human," he said.

"Too many reasons for that," I said.

Of course, I admired Schuyler for having wept. Man that he was. But I had another feeling too, in my tears. I remembered that life was vicious, and at this rate I was going to go through it with no one to help me.

I didn't say anything, and at night I was more eager than ever, quite the little she-wolf in bed, because I had given up entirely. There was nothing for me; this was the last of it, whatever it was. I was mired in defeat and angry too. Schuyler knew something was up but he didn't exactly know what. "It was an intense day," he said, before he fell asleep. What kind of crap was that?

I kept us from turning against each other in the time we had left, but it took effort. The last night of the shoot, the whole crew had a big huge meal in the caterer's tent. There was a drizzly summer rain outside as it grew darker. People were getting drunk and saying how great we all were. Schuyler said to me, "I'll miss you, you know."

Throw the dog a bone? He couldn't do better than that?

"You'll be fine," I said. "I'm not worried about you."

He looked pained at this, and he took my hand and kissed it. Which annoyed me. I went home with him that night anyway, but I was deciding I didn't completely like him. Who knew if he even noticed?

So that was that. I went back to my old job leading people to their seats at a theater in town, and I was lucky the place took me back. Between acts I had too much time to obsess and I tried not to. I had a whole long life ahead of me, at the mercy of who knew what, and I was going to need powers of distance, if nothing else. Easier said than done, of course.

And it turned out I was in for two surprises. One, emails from Schuyler appeared within days. *Hi, Maribel. Thinking of you. Just had great meal at Egyptian restaurant, no wonder you want to move there.* He was trying to be chatty. *How are you?*

Surprise two was that the producers were not at all satisfied with certain parts of the film and were sending the crew back to Leeds for two weeks to reshoot. Soon. I heard this at the pub and everybody said, "Well, don't look too excited or anything. Look at her." In the morning he sent a message with *hip hip hooray* in the subject line.

It was a miracle, wasn't it, but why did we have to depend on miracles? The American crew got off the plane together, and I was one of the people directing them from the luggage pickup to the transit vans we'd arranged. The sight of Schuyler hit my heart like three thousand grams of caffeine—look at him, it was Schuyler—and he crossed over to give me a quick, comradely hug. "Later," he whispered.

Once we got ourselves alone, we were like a couple making up after a fight, although we hadn't fought—we were sobered and chastened and on fire. The crew was full of group jokes about how the two of us never left the hotel room. But that was not even the point. The point had to do with gratitude. What if we had lost all this?

The filming itself was tenser this time—they had to get right whatever it was they'd gotten wrong—and the director, Tara, went into scornful mode. I tried to get Schuyler away from the crew at day's end, just for relief, and I decided we could spend some nights at my place. Despite my flatmate.

"That's a nice watch," Emilia said to him. "You don't look super-posh except for your watch." We were sitting around the kitchen drinking shots of gin before we went to bed.

"Will you please?" I said.

"It's all right," Schuyler said. "I like the watch too."

"Who made the money?" Emilia said. "Grandparents? Great-grandparents?"

"Great-grand," Schuyler said. "He was an itinerant salesman in Colorado. There's a legend that he cheated his partner."

"Anyone who's made a huge amount of money," Emilia said, "did harm to get it. Everybody knows."

"You think so?" Schuyler turned to ask me.

"I guess I do," I said.

"Maribel's father is no better," Emilia said. "But he fell on his ass. A lesson there."

My father, who'd been a software engineer for different multinationals in the Middle East, had invested in something unwise. He now lived in a bedsit in London and drank too much.

"Maybe I'll meet him someday," Schuyler said. That was new.

On the way to work the next morning he spoke for the first time about his wife. A perfectly nice person, Veronica, but she sort of never did anything. He hadn't known she'd be like that. I had no pity for the wife at all. It was her own fault she wasn't as consistently interesting as I was.

"You'd like America," he started saying. Would I? But I was glad to hear him say it.

My mother told me men with money could be bossy. We had this conversation on the phone, since I wasn't getting myself across town to visit her. We meant well but we got on each other's nerves.

"I hope you know that if he leaves his wife," my mum said, "that probably means he'll leave you someday."

No wonder I neglected her. I wasn't letting Schuyler meet her either. He sort of thought she was in London.

"I never meant to stay in Leeds," I said. "Maybe I'll just go to Cairo."

"You don't really think I believe you," she said, "do you?"

People could rain on our parade all they wanted, but Schuyler was becoming more smitten with me. None of my other boyfriends had gotten to the stage he was in. In bed when I was dozing off I'd open my eyes and see him gazing at me, taking in the sight of me. Was he kidding himself? A man who still wore a ring?

"You'd get a kick out of Coney Island," he said one night, when we were in my kitchen with no Emilia around. "Like Brighton only much funkier. I can't wait to show you New York."

"Do you plan to hide me until you get rid of your nice wife?" I said.

"No! Don't say that," he said. "No one is hiding you."

"What then?"

"We'll work it out. It can be done. Give me time."

What the fuck did that mean?

"You think you can have everything you want," I said.

He looked surprised that this was an accusation. "You worry too much," he said. "Keep calm."

I had understood Schuyler as a gentle and easygoing person. I'd never seen him before as confident in a rotten way. Or close to that.

"You think I'll just arrive on your shores, like magic," I said.

"Maribel. I'll send you a ticket. You're not worried about the ticket?"

Oh, we were on to money already?

"Send me a first-class ticket," I said. "No, send me my own private jet."

"What is it with you?" he said.

"Send me a golden spaceship," I said.

"Could you stop being my enemy for a second?" he said.

And then I decided that maybe I could stop; what was I doing?

My position was not good in this thing. The day before, we'd been eating some kind of pudding from the food truck, and he said, "I have to say, Veronica makes a really great key lime pie."

"Your wife."

"Yeah, her. She does apple too."

"That's wonderful," I said.

"She can do coconut sticky rice too. She used to have a Thai boyfriend."

"Lovely," I said.

End of discussion. If he was longing for her desserts, he could keep it to himself.

I saw, not for the first time, where I had gotten myself, the wide pit of misery I could be walking straight into. Why had no one warned me? Well, my mother had, but who'd pay attention to her? She once believed my father was so shrewd about money we'd soon be living in a mansion in London. She used to laugh at how witless the other engineers in Doha were, missing their chance. That was how much she knew.

The thing about Schuyler was, he didn't know his own mind. I thought I had a stronger personality than his wife—I loomed larger as long as I was next to him. But once I wasn't with him, I could seem like a mere trick of light, a mistaken impression. We loved each other, privately and well, but everyone knows how love vanishes.

I had to be much more careful, in this very delicate and critical stage. I had to stop fucking things up. Did I think men like Schuyler grew on trees? They didn't, I knew that.

✦ ✦ ✦

Two nights later we were in the back of the pub, eating our snacks in the lounge. Schuyler was especially famished because he'd gone off to smoke something or other with Alastair, and he was eating all the chips from my plate when the phone in his pocket went off. Without a word to anyone, he walked off to take the call outside, and he was gone a good twenty minutes. This had not happened before; it was probably his wife, who had every right to call him. He was lying to her at this moment, telling her he missed her. Maybe that wasn't a lie either.

Whatever we did in bed he'd had years to play out with another body. He never said he hated her. One of the caterer's cooks had a T-shirt that said, *I taught your boyfriend that thing you like.* Was that the caption for the cartoon that was my life? I felt mocked by everything around me. The crew guys at the table looked at me awkwardly while Schuyler was outside.

"Sorry," he said, when he came back.

"Good conversation?" I said.

"It was my stupid credit card company. It's earlier there."

He had never lied to me, as far as I knew, but did I know anything?

"You might try to make up a better one," I said.

"Please don't start. I have to argue with morons about my credit balance, and I have to deal with you too?"

"You don't *have* to deal with me," I said. "No one is making you."

"You get hostile when you drink," he said. "I've noticed this."

I said I didn't think he noticed anything. And I could drink whatever I wanted. Who was he to say? "Since when are my phone calls a threat to you?" he said.

"Maybe you think I'm an idiot," I said. "You always thought so." We had never fought in front of other people before.

"Keep your voice down," he said, but everyone heard. He was never leaving his wife; I saw that now. Why had it taken me so long? I was the one who said, "Never mind," and I went home, and he didn't try to keep me from leaving either.

In the middle of the night my phone rang—I wasn't letting Schuyler get me out of bed for more fake stories and bullshit arguing—and I turned the thing to silent and went back to sleep. I woke up at six the next day with a fierce headache, and Emilia had eaten all the breakfast food in the house—forget toast, even the tea was gone. I made it over to the hotel feeling very peckish indeed; the good news was that the big buffet still had piles of the bacon I liked, and Schuyler wasn't there yet. "You think they'll bring more sausage?" I said to Kerry, one of the set dressers.

"You can eat?" she said. "Maybe that's a good thing. I guess the hospital doesn't have much at this hour."

"What hospital?"

"Oh, Maribel," she said. "You don't know."

I had slept all through Schuyler's leaving the pub by himself and crossing the street right in the path of an SUV going in what must have seemed like the wrong direction to him. A big SUV. He still wasn't conscious yet, he had a lot wrong with him, ribs and something in his chest—they would see, they would know soon. She was still talking when I ran out, with half-chewed bacon still in my mouth, and tried to use my phone to get a cab. I made no sense, my voice wasn't my voice, and when the taxi really came, I shouted *yes*, as if everything was fine now.

Whoever the doctors were talking to in the hospital, it wasn't me. There was a cluster of people I knew in the waiting room, and Tara, the director, came out from the room to talk to us all. I was shushing everybody so I could hear her. The family, she said, was arranging for the body to be sent back to the U.S., the hospital knew how to do this, there were legal hassles but they knew the procedures. *The body?*

I made a noise like a yelp, and Alastair took my arm. And

then we all had to leave; there was nothing to stay for. "I just got here!" I said. No one would tell me where he was in the hospital. People hugged me, people I liked; they were kind to me, and they were leading me out. Nothing to stay for.

I didn't even know where to go. I went back to the hotel with the others, and somebody had tea brought out to us. "They don't know anything about the driver, do they?" Kerry said. Whatever anyone was saying was crazy and petty and very, very beside the point. I couldn't really hear them anyway. Everything in the ongoing world was empty and beneath consideration and always had been, a big fuss over nothing. I was surrounded by the noise of nothing.

Alastair, who hovered over me as if I needed tending, which I did, walked me back to my flat. "We had a fight," I said. Then we were in my room with Schuyler's newspapers and socks on the floor, and he smoothed out all my bed sheets so I could, as he said, have a good rest. "We had a fight," I said again. Did I want him to call anyone? Not my mother, I was thinking, not yet.

"I'm so sorry," he said. Everyone said.

And so Schuyler vanished from my life as entirely as if he'd been erased. The crew sent a card to his wife, and I signed the card, and that was the last I had to do with him in any outward way. No need to make claims for what he'd been to me; why would I want to do that to the wife? It was fine to be invisible. That wasn't the part I minded.

The shoot went on again after two days' delay, as it had to. An actor stood in front of Armley Mills and quoted Charles Dickens, who apparently called Leeds "an odious place." I knew the actor—he was local, his brother had once painted my mother's house—and the director gave him a hard time over those few measly lines. They were ready to go home, all of them.

And they did go. Alastair and I helped shepherd them to the airport with all their equipment, which they had too much of. Why had they brought all that? They were in a great tizzy, the whole lot, pesky and loud and getting in the way. With their nasal American voices, their worry about aisle seats and legroom.

Once we were gone from them, returning one of the rental vans, Alastair said to me, "You want food? I think we should get you food."

He and his boyfriend had been plying me with snacks, coaxing me to try to rest. Even Emilia and my mother had done their awkward best. I appreciated this; I needed them, I knew I did. But they persisted in chattering on about the world, which they were still in. Alastair had to talk about how Tara, the director, was getting a name for herself; not many women directors, and she was a tiger, wasn't she? Emilia had to obsess about how Barack Obama was so much sexier than David Cameron, what was wrong with the U.K., and my mother was worried about the vine weevils running amok in her garden, weevils were invading England. I didn't give a fuck about any of it, how could I, and I held them all in secret contempt for going on as if any of it had any importance whatsoever. They kept at it, wearing themselves out, exaggerating what didn't matter at all. I half heard what they said, I let them go on, and I saw through what they couldn't see through. I thought they were all infants.

They helped me all the time. And because of them I was ashamed to simply hide and sleep; I got up in the morning, I went back to my old menial job as an usher. It was a job you could be stupid at, if you went through the motions. Probably most things were like that.

My mother fed me lunches and had me working in her garden, dabbing from a jar of sticky goo onto papers wrapped around the bases of plants. Why did she think being the death squad for weevils would cheer me? She had opinions about Schuyler, whom she'd never met. "It was from having all that money," she said, "that he walked right out into that street as if it were his."

"I'd appreciate your not talking," I said.

"You'll feel better once you find someone else," she said. "Of course, you won't find anyone with as much money as he had."

My father had been a boy of twenty-seven, already earning a good salary in the Emirates, when I was born. She still complained about my father, and also about a much younger man she was sort of dating, who didn't seem that crazy about her. "Your father always loved gardens," she said. "I don't know how he lives now in a room without a window."

In Qatar, we lived in a big, glassy place we rented. My father admired the local mastery of a desert climate under air-conditioned domes and arcades; it thrilled his engineer's heart. These days he lived in a room only just big enough for a bed, loo down the hall, shared kitchen.

My father had been in his bedsit for five years, the longest of anyone in his building. He said people in the other bedsits came to see him, to find out how to get the hot water back up and how to get the fridge door to shut right. "My knowledge is appreciated," he said. Some were grateful enough to leave him a bottle of whiskey when they moved out; it had become a custom. "I prefer whiskey to gin, but not everyone is clever enough to ask." My dear father had become a figure out of Dickens—he was the man in *Little Dorrit* who settles into Marshalsea debtors' prison for twenty years, greeting newcomers, explaining he's called the father of the Marshalsea, expecting small cash tributes when they leave.

For all that my mother and I laughed at it, my father's vanity had sustained him—kept him from coming apart entirely—when all else failed. Now he had the role of a faded colonial to fall into, talking about his glory days in the Emirates and Qatar. Sometimes I did that too, in my way, dropping words in Arabic into any reminiscence of my teen years.

But what kind of life had we had? Our Nepali housekeeper, Binsa, had not seen her own family for nine years. Our stunning apartment complex had been built by men from South Asia and Africa who lived in sweltering camps and couldn't leave until their contracts expired. We were no better than the fat cats in Dickens's day, insisting they could never compete if they gave the workers more. How had we pretended not to notice? We sort of had.

And neither of my parents had come out of that sealed luxury with so much as a shilling to show for it. My mother worked part-time in a preschool these days and was poorly paid. "I need to plant more vegetables while I can," she was telling me. "That's the way to save." She said the man she'd been dating was wild for her aubergine curry—could aubergine grow here? "He admires my cooking, even when he's too busy to come by and eat it. There's too much busyness nowadays."

"There is," I said. I let her go on about the terribly packed schedule of her important new friend. She had no idea how she sounded.

"I bet you find someone soon," she said. "You'll be surprised."

My parents' marriage had split up when the money ran out. Perhaps that was putting it harshly—my mother had been sorely disappointed not just in their lost income but in my father's character, his fraudulent claims about his shrewdness. Also his drinking. Neither of them had much to say now that was useful about how I was to go on, with Schuyler gone. Sometimes my mother said, "You really hadn't been with him that long." This was true, but it was the opposite of comforting.

"You have all this time ahead of you," she said, and I didn't like that either.

When I first got the job as an usher, I thought it was a great perk that I got to see plays over and over. I had ambitions to write a screenplay someday. At the end of whatever was onstage, serious or light, I would look around me, amazed that I was still in Leeds, behind seated rows of spectators, not in the plot of whatever had been acted out.

For a month now they had been doing *Antony and Cleopatra*—tale of a doomed man with a dull wife in Rome and a fabulous woman left behind in Alexandria. I was definitely on Cleopatra's side. The sets for Cleopatra's palace had gold and purple draperies and a sexy divan. I had never been to Alexandria—maybe it was where I should be moving, not Cairo. As if any of my plans meant anything, as if I could really go anywhere.

I formed a new habit of slipping off to an alcove above the stairs, where they let ushers sit as long as we kept quiet; we still had to hear the actors shouting and laughing and giving long, rippling speeches (what hams they were). Everything felt like mere clamor to me now. Sometimes I rested in this feeling. People thought I was just plain out of it these days, a moron of grief, but I had glimpses of how there might be a freedom in it too.

I wasn't much good to anyone all those months. I didn't join in when Alastair discussed the decline of British film; I was a poor audience when Emilia explained how the Scottish National Party was really postmodern. I edged away from too much talk; I could hardly hear people. That was just the way it was.

Did I feel superior to everyone and their topics of concern? Well, yes. Why was I so sure that death had made me smarter? I liked my floaty superior life more than I could have admitted. I was different and better. I liked the remote spaces I was settling into; I liked looking from above. I kept this preference to myself, mostly.

In the spring Alastair got a few months' work on a TV series in London, and he commuted back on weekends with gossip. Tara, our old director, hadn't been satisfied with what she'd shot in Leeds, and she had decided the film needed a whole other half. "History is smug," she said. "We always think we're better now." And she had talked the producers into sending her to Bangladesh to talk to current-day workers in garment factories. "Remember when that factory complex in Bangladesh collapsed," Alastair said, "after the owners knew the building was fucked and made hundreds of workers go in? That's where she went, some place near there. She did that already."

"Leeds and Bangladesh, together at last," Max said.

"It's Leeds and Dhaka. Dhaka is the city," Alastair said. He was all up into the thing, as if it were his project.

I looked up the factory collapse near Dhaka. The workers were paid so little, the Pope himself had called it slave labor. Which the world was full of, still. Tara was not wrong.

Qatar was built on another version of such labor, with its Nepali road crews who turned in their passports and couldn't leave, its indentured Filipina maids.

The next thing we heard about the film was that it was having its long-awaited debut—first public showing—at a festival in Brooklyn in the autumn. Brooklyn!

"We should go," I said. "It's not that far, New York. Why not?"

"All that way to see a movie?" Max said. "We're not the stars."

"There is no star. It's a documentary," Alastair said.

"Don't you want to see how it turned out?" I said. Brooklyn. I knew where Schuyler's street was—I could go walk on that street. I just wanted to see it.

Of course, none of us had the money to take off just like that. We looked at airfares; we counted up the work days we'd miss. Neither of them wanted to go as much as I did, and maybe it was a pathetic idea, looking at footage my lover had taken when he was a live person. Anyway, none of us went.

But we read a review. Max googled and found it in local coverage of the festival. "Humans haven't gotten any better," the reviewer wrote, "in the past century and a half. The sad exploitation of textile and garment workers is depicted in really quite stunning images in this odd but intriguing film, with its double vision of then and now."

"*Stunning* is good," Alastair said.

I said, "I wonder if his family knows."

Schuyler's family had never been impressed by his career choice. I wanted them to see how well he had done. If not the parents, at least his brothers. Tad and Richard; I knew their names, I knew that much.

Were they on Facebook? Tad was. In the picture he was on a boat, rowing on a lake. He looked stockier than Schuyler.

He friended me back in a day. I messaged him to say I'd known Schuyler in England, sent him a link to the review. *Dear Maribel*, he wrote back. *Quite a surprise to hear from you. We have all wondered about you. Are you available to have a chat on the phone?*

Schuyler had talked about me? We set up a time in the late afternoon and I was beside myself imagining Schuyler treating me as a topic. I couldn't believe it when the phone really rang. "Hello," Tad said. "We speak at last." The voice was a lot like Schuyler's, which was weird.

I asked how he was, and he grunted about how impossible retail was now but I must know that. "I've wanted to speak to you," he said. "What I really need, if you don't mind, is information about when Schuyler left the pub and walked into the street. Did you see?"

What a horrifying question. "Oh, no. I'd gone home already."

"It's the life insurance. We're having trouble collecting it."

The parents had bought policies for each of the sons when they'd come into the trust. The brothers were the beneficiaries of one another. Schuyler had failed to inform the insurance company about his use of recreational drugs, present in his system at time of death.

"Did you give him the drugs?" Tad asked.

"What? No."

"Was he stoned all the time? You can say so. I know Schuyler could be a real fuckup."

"He was very talented," I said, a little loudly.

"Was there a reason," Tad said, "you left the pub first? If you'd been crossing the street with him, he'd have gotten to the other side."

I thought that every day, but it wasn't Tad's business to say it. They still hadn't settled the insurance, a year and four months after Schuyler's death?

"If a witness could say that he looked both ways," Tad said, "collecting on the policy would be a lot easier."

"I'm sorry," I said. "I wasn't there. People saw me leave."

"What people?"

Did he plan to pay them off? What a seedy scheme. I wasn't dragging my friends into this.

"Too many," I said.

"Try to think," he said. He waited through my silence on the phone.

"Schuyler was never going to leave his wife, you know," he said. "No matter what he told you. He was always *almost* leaving and then staying with Veronica. You weren't his first." What was remarkable about this speech was that his voice was cracking. He was ready to hit something or start weeping: he had loved Schuyler.

And the brothers wanted money. Oh, why not. The story about the wife was supposed to answer a question I hardly had anymore. I had wandered away from that question—far and away, left it behind. I was used to the blunt fact of Schuyler's dying. The endless obduracy of it. A fact as pure as the moon. What did I care about Veronica? What could the poor woman take from me now?

"Schuyler would want you to help me," Tad said. He was trying another tack.

"Schuyler's gone," I said.

He would've heard this as cold, but I was trying to get us on a higher plane. I wondered (as I had before) what sort of funeral they'd had for him. What the brothers had said, whether poor Veronica had wept. Now Tad was stuck on the insurance, the golden hoard, as if it were his one chance at happiness. He was hoping very hard for it, over and over. I was his hope! What a vain little errand he'd given himself.

"Please convey my very best regards to your whole family," I said. "You know I wish you all well." Did I? Tad didn't say a thing.

"Glad we got to talk," I said, and that was the end of it.

I was sorry I hadn't given him a harder time. I might've voiced my lack of pity for uncollected death benefits. I might've reminded him that I hadn't pushed his brother into the road.

"Did he call just to insult you?" Alastair said, when I told him the whole story.

"I'm sure he thought he could draw me in," I said. "That I'd want the money too. He had, you know, financial delusions."

"Which you are free of," Max said.

"It's the hugeness of the family company," Alastair said, "makes them expect more."

Max said, "Company's going under."

"Exactly," I said. "All built on sand. I know about family misinvestments."

"I love it when you take the long view," Alastair said.

The truth was, Schuyler was fading a little in my head. I thought of him every day but I'd lost the sense he was just out of sight. I did want to complain to him now, *Can you believe what Tad said to me?* And I naturally would've pointed out to him too, if I could have, the magnificent self-restraint I had just displayed over the phone. Where was he? *I kept calm,* I would've said to him, *and carried on fine, in case you want to know.*

In the days after that phone call, I was often giving long speeches in my mind, explaining why I hadn't crossed the street with Schuyler. Who was I explaining to? Actually, the person I kept thinking of was Veronica. I had no way to picture her, of course, but I knew very well how the savage shock of the news must've hit her, how hollow the months after must've been. I hoped she was better—I was better—did she want to hear this? I was perfectly sure she'd had her own high impatience with the petty inconsequential garbage people couldn't stop going on about, the small-beyond-small concerns they were stuck in. How they went on. We could've talked about that and felt quite free together.

4 / Rachel

MY BROTHER'S LONGTIME BOYFRIEND DECIDED TO leave him, once and for all. Enough, he said, was enough. If you can't stop arguing after twenty years, when will you ever? Time for a new start for both of them. They would always be friends, of course. He would always care about Saul, but he did not think that waking up every day in the same apartment was good for either of them.

This speech might have made sense except that my brother had just been diagnosed with some stage or other of leukemia. (Lymphocytic leukemia, and it was hard to get a full story out of Saul.) And the apartment, in the upper reaches of Manhattan, belonged to Kirk, the boy-friend. My brother, a fifty-seven-year-old librarian with no personal savings, was going to have to find a new place to live. For however long he planned to do that.

I was stunned and outraged by the news, maybe more than my brother was. Why had I ever liked Kirk? I had, I always had. With his deep voice, his good haircuts, his quiet merciless jokes. He called me Sister Susie (my name is

Rachel, the name was his kidding). Sister Susie was a perky lass, always getting into the gin on the sly. We had a whole set of stories about her and her unusual relations with her dog Spot. Some of his friends thought I was really called Susie.

How could you decide to break up with someone who had a mortal illness? Who could do such a thing? Kirk could.

"The man is a fuck-head," I said to Saul. "And he has no honor."

"We never got along that well," Saul said. "Remember when he picked a fight with me in front of the entire Brooklyn Library staff? He was always a pain. And you know how full of himself he's been. He thinks being a digital art director is like being Michelangelo—I always laughed at the way he used the word *creative*. Don't make a big deal out of this. It's not the end of the world."

What is, then? I thought, but I didn't say it.

Kirk had not given him any particular deadline for moving out, and everyone in New York knew couples who stayed together for years after breaking up, while prices rose and good deals slipped away. Meanwhile Kirk and my brother were sharing the same bed every night and were—I gleaned from my brother's remarks—still having what could be called sexual contact. I didn't blame Saul for mentioning it either, showing off a last bit of swagger.

And maybe the breakup was just an idea, a flash-in-the pan theory. Maybe Kirk didn't mean it.

"He says I'm lazy about being sick," Saul said. "I should do more, be proactive. Has anyone used that word since 1997?"

"What is it with him?" I said. "I don't get it."

"He's seeing someone new," Saul said.

"He's *what?*" I said. I had to stop wailing in protest, because it was useless and only increased my brother's suffering. He had his ties to Kirk; he didn't want to hear what I had to say. *No big deal* was his mantra, and there was probably a way to say it in Sanskrit or Pali. "It's someone named Ethan," Saul said. "A lawyer." Did I want to know his name? I did not.

I was his big sister, two years older, but we were both old now. I was the one with the more chaotic sexual history—I'd been with a long list of men and lived with some very poor choices—but time had passed since those days. The daughter of one of my boyfriends (I was never into marriage) still lived with me, after losing patience with both her parents, and she was already twenty-three. I loved Nadia, I was glad to have her with me, but my apartment wasn't really one that could fit her and me and my brother too. An old bargain of a place in Hell's Kitchen. Not that Saul had expressed any interest in moving in.

Was he looking at apartments? Not at the moment. At the moment he was busy going to a clinic where they inserted a needle into a port in his arm and dripped chemicals into his veins. I went with him for this—it was not an adorable procedure—and it took a while. Nadia went to pick him up once. And Kirk went the rest of the time. He did.

Saul would go home to sleep after the procedures—who wouldn't?—and he'd lie around with headphones on watching Netflix for hours when sleep evaded him. The library was giving him time off with no trouble, and maybe he was never going back. He hadn't shown any improvement after the first round of chemo, and the doctors wanted to start something else. He was still losing weight; his nose looked bigger, outgrowing his face. It hurt my heart to look at him. "He could *try* to eat," Kirk said. "He doesn't even try. I buy things he likes, that he always liked. You know he likes those pecan crunch things. It doesn't matter."

I had my own life, of course, my own work, my own loyalties. I had a decent-enough job in human resources for a hotel chain, overseeing stingy policies and crazy rate changes. I was the old girl who'd been there forever and knew the ropes. Nadia liked to ask if I could game the system—get billions paid out in insurance for someone who was healthy—but I had to tell her that was beyond me. Nadia had a youthful attitude about the possibilities of cheating. Anyway, one night I was buying us supper at her favorite Mexican place in the West Village when I heard someone at a nearby table say, "Just be patient. Okay?"

I knew the voice; it was Kirk's. He was talking to a nice-looking dude in his forties, arguing in that weary, reasonable way of his. I knew that tone. It must be his new lover, this not-so-happy guy in a dark suit.

"I've been waiting a while," the guy said.

Oh, were they waiting for my brother to die? Or just to disappear, to crawl offstage? I was choking with fury. Did I want to rush over and make a scene? Did I want to stay where I was to hear more?

"Hey!" Nadia said, solving the problem for me. "There's Kirk! Hey, Kirk!"

He took in the sight of us, waved. What a fuck-head. "Look at you," he called out to Nadia, across two tables in between. "You're looking great. Hi, Rachel. This is my friend, Ethan."

We all nodded at one another.

Even Nadia was taking things in. "Why does everybody all of a sudden know about this restaurant?" she said. "I hate the way it is now, all these people."

"Everybody knows everything nowadays," Kirk said.

"Not for the better either," I said.

"We had a very nice meal," Kirk said. "Didn't you think

so, Ethan? We're almost done. Don't mind us. Enjoy your drinks."

And then he turned away from us and murmured something to Ethan. He could go ahead and pretend they were in another room; he could do what he wanted.

"They'll leave soon," I said to Nadia. Not that softly either.

Around us a speaker was playing, "*Besame, besame mucho.*" The singer was pleading in long notes. We stood our ground; we chewed and drank. Nadia said, "I can't believe he had to bring him here." I didn't know they had left until, halfway through my second bottle of Dos Equis, I looked across and spotted other diners at that table.

"He thinks he's so slick," she said. "Mr. Not-Embarrassed."

"He's like Woody Allen—the heart wants what it wants. Remember when he said that when he ran off with his stepdaughter?" Nadia had probably not even been born then, but she'd heard about it. "People think if they're honest about their cravings, it makes anything okay," I said. "That's a fallacy of modern life."

I found out Nadia was doing what sounded like praying for my brother. She hadn't been raised in any religion (not with those parents), but she was a great reader online, she taught herself things. In the middle of the night I was in the hallway on my way to pee, when I heard her voice in the living room. "May Saul be better," I heard. "May he be well and happy. May he live with ease. May he live longer."

And Who did she think was processing this request? I didn't ask. I didn't want to smudge the purity of whatever she was doing. I listened for her again as I walked down that hallway the night after, but no words vibrated in the air. The next morning, when I got up early, I saw that she slept (as always) flat on her back on the folded-out sofa, and the statue of the Buddha had been moved to a shelf in her line of sight. It was Saul's Buddha—that is, he had brought it to me after a trip somewhere. Thailand? Cambodia? It was a gray stone figure, the size of a gallon of milk, sitting with one hand raised with a flat palm. Fear not, that hand gesture meant. Saul had been a fan of Buddhism—he read books, he went to meditation classes, he explained very well how ego-craving was the source of all suffering—but his interest had faded in the last few years. He hadn't said anything about leaning on it now. But Nadia was?

"You don't have to follow all the rules," she said, when I asked. "People get so caught up in that. As if somebody twenty-five hundred years ago was the last one to know anything about spiritual matters. How could that be right?" What I'd heard as prayer were phrases from a Buddhist practice, but she had added flourishes, like setting out a green ribbon (I hadn't noticed) because Saul's favorite color was green.

At least she wasn't kneeling. When I was a child, my mother caught me kneeling by my bed, intoning, "Now I lay me down to sleep, I pray the Lord my soul to keep." (How did I even know that prayer?)

"Jews don't kneel," my mother said.

I got up right away. I sort of loved the urgency in my mother's voice. She spoke rarely about religious matters and sometimes made fun of what I learned in Hebrew School. This was serious. I wanted serious; that was why I was praying.

Like Nadia. All over the world (I traveled much in my wayward youth), people go in for petitionary prayer; they ask for concrete and specific things, even when they're not supposed to, according to their systems of belief. They set out flowers, fruit, candles, money. Tiny models of body parts they want fixed. Votive wishes on papers they pin on trees.

I looked at the green ribbon, a strip of satin left over from a Christmas package. Did she think a higher power could bring about what she wanted? "You never know," she said.

"Can't argue with that," I said, though I could have.

✦ ✦ ✦

Nadia was nine when I first met her. I was dating Nick, her dad, and he had her on weekends. She kept calling me by the wrong name on purpose—Rochelle, Raybelle, Michelle—and looking at me with fiendish eyes. But she got over all that, eventually, and then she was nuzzling and cuddling like a much younger kid and saying she liked my house. She pocketed a spoon when she left. (I saw, who cared?) I admired her resourcefulness, her range of attempts to be on top of the situation. She was working hard to watch out for herself. When her father later referred to her as a total pill—he liked that phrase—I said, "What kind of crap is that?"

Now it was Saul's turn to be a total pill. He talked too much about his different kinds of chemo; he talked too much about his white blood cells. Once he had been happy to argue about how detective novels were good for the brains of middle school kids and why online reading was a triumph against capitalism. Now he was like any patient, caught up in the drama of his own ordeals, his schedule of medications, the textures of his shrinking world. I wanted him to be better than that.

"Sister Susie says you should have a joint," I said. "Your treatments are over. You can do what you want." I lit up while I was spreading this doctrine.

"What *do* I fucking want?" he said. But he took a hit. "There's nothing I want."

"Isn't that an ideal state in Buddhism?" I said.

"That's a gross simplification," Saul said. But he looked at least a little pleased. It was better news than he'd heard for a while.

"Did you know Nadia's been chanting on your behalf?"

"She told me," he said. "What a good girl she turned into."

He really wanted nothing? He had to want to live, if he was going to last a little longer. Indifference would drag him under. What did nothing mean? Maybe I wasn't paying attention properly.

Before my brother's diagnosis, my life had been in what felt like a good phase. Two crucial areas had shown improvement. An ex-boyfriend—everyone called him Bud—who'd left New York eight years before had started sending me emails. He'd gone off to Cambodia to work for an NGO, defending workers' rights, which clearly needed defending, there and here. We'd parted badly but we always remembered each other's birthdays, which was mature of us. On my last birthday, he'd written, *Hands across the water, hands across the sky,* lines to a song that had been popular in middle school. Once Bud started writing, I was always humming it in my head. And finally, at long last, Nadia seemed to be out of the woods—she'd left behind her habits of moping and quitting and having fits of fury and bouts of despair and going a little nuts. She was back in school, taking computer design classes at FIT that she liked to talk about; she was sane. I walked around feeling secretly smug, as if I'd been right about everything all along.

Which at least made it easier to be nice to Saul when he uttered the same complaints over and over. "I'm nauseated all the time," he said. "I hate it. I can't even barf. I can't do anything."

"You can't read?" I said. He was a librarian, for Christ's sake. The original escapist reader. Thrilled by discoveries, an enthusiast of hidden corners of information. "You want some audiobooks? You could be nauseous and listen at the same time."

"Never mind," he said. "You don't get it."

We were having this conversation in the bedroom of his and Kirk's apartment. He was sitting up in bed, wrapped in a blanket. He'd shaved his head, and it wasn't a flattering look. The night table was a mess of pill bottles, old socks. Did he maybe want to smoke something? "It doesn't help," he said. "Why do people say it helps?"

Kirk was in the living room, tapping on his cell phone. He called out to Saul, "You know there's some of that mango smoothie in the fridge. Easy to swallow. Don't you think you would like that?"

"Why do you think I would like anything?" Saul said.

"Silly me," Kirk said.

Meanwhile, in the midst of this, Bud the old boyfriend had decided it was time for us to Skype each other—Phnom Penh to NYC. Hands across the water. "Rachel!" he said, when we were on each other's screens. I always loved his voice. It was Bud! His hair was shorter, grayer (so was mine but dyed). Had he always had that slight web under his chin? "Isn't this weird, this teledating?" he said. Oh, we were dating? I could see the room behind him, a beaded curtain over a closet, an open window with green palm fronds outside.

"Is it hot there now?" I said. "It's snowing here."

"It's in the eighties. You'd like it. You like summer."

I'd been to parts of Southeast Asia when I was a restless young thing—Thailand and Malaysia—but people weren't going to Cambodia then, a postwar mess even to backpackers. "It's still a mess," he said.

"It's a mess here too," I said. I had already told him my worst Trump jokes. "The rich get richer. *You* know."

"What amazes me in my line of work," he said, "is the strength of people to go on." He had these moments of grandstanding but his points were good. "You see them come out of these factories where they work ten hours a day in suffocating heat, wages so low they can barely eat, and sometimes a girl is laughing at what her friend said. Too tired to move but something is still funny."

I was wondering if Bud could kid around with them in whatever language they spoke. "Khmer," he said. "Khmer is Cambodian. It can take them a while to see I'm being funny on purpose."

He probably wasn't as hilarious as he imagined. "You should come visit," he said. "Come to Phnom Penh."

"Sure," I said, as if he really meant it, which I didn't think he did. As if I could go anytime, just like that.

I was at my desk at work when my brother called with a piece of startling news. "Guess what I did?" he said. "I ate a huge bowl of mint chip ice cream. Two and a half scoops. I'm feeling better."

"Icy cold? Is that okay?"

"Went down fine. I might have more."

I laughed. "You were hungry."

"Maybe those needle jabs are working. Maybe I'm getting better. I feel better."

"You do?"

"I don't get that tired when I walk around either. I just wanted to tell you."

"I'm so glad."

"Two and a half scoops. I might have more."

I couldn't believe it—I was too happy to stay still, so I was strolling around the room with the phone. Maybe he had more time than we thought. He hadn't done well at first but maybe he was on an upswing. He could be.

Later that night, Nadia said, "Well, it was *supposed* to work. That's why he did it."

"*Supposed to* doesn't usually mean shit," I said, and then I was sorry I had spoken like that to a young person.

"If he's better," my friend Amy at work said, "then you can run off to Cambodia. Have sex with your ex, see Angkor Wat."

"It's too far. You know how far away it is? Twenty hours by plane. At the very least."

"I guess you looked online," she said.

And the airfare wasn't nothing either. Or did Bud think he was paying? We hadn't gotten anywhere near that question.

"Everyone's leaving my brother," I said. "I don't have to join them."

"So I found this nice little apartment," my brother said. "Small, but small isn't bad. Decent light."

"You were looking?" I said. "I didn't know you were looking." This made me worry what else I had missed.

"Well, it fell into my lap," he said.

"It's affordable? Really?" Was it over a sewage plant? In nearby Nevada?

"It's in our building," Saul said. "Our neighbor has this studio he wants to sublet."

It was just three floors down.

"This guy wants a big deposit," Saul said. "People do now. Two months' security, one month in advance. I don't know where he thinks I'd be skipping away to. Kirk is lending me the money."

Lend, my ass. My brother's lover was paying him to leave. And they'd be greeting each other in the elevator forever. And everybody was acting cheerful about it.

"I'm looking forward to having my own place," Saul said. "It's been years since I had that."

"Did you want to be alone?"

"No," he said. "But it's fine."

Nadia thought her meditating had brought about this improvement for Saul, her focusing on the words with all her strength. Something had gotten him better, against all odds. "I did more than you know. Most of it not out loud," she said. "Don't laugh."

"I'm not laughing."

"What's the other reason? There isn't any."

I wasn't offering any details of science. She looked so happy. She was still an awkward girl, and happiness made her face rounder and bolder.

"Saul thanked me," she said. "He said I was amazing."

My brother's character was improving, now that he was on an upward swing. Sick people had crappy dispositions. "He wants me to design something for the windows of his new place," Nadia said. "I can do that."

Was he going back to work? He'd always had a ridiculously long commute, from Inwood at the top of Manhattan all the way south to Brooklyn, an hour and fifteen minutes, but he used to say he liked reading on the subway. He had an unimpressive salary, decent insurance (I had checked it over), and not that bad a pension. Did he want to be in the library again?

He wasn't saying. He didn't even like it when we asked. When he was little, he loved to announce, "That's for me to know and you to find out," and he seemed to want to say that now. "Later for that," he muttered. To *me*, he said this.

My mother always claimed everyone thought Saul was less stubborn than he really was. I got along better with my mother than he did, and I had trouble too. We lost both our parents, within months of each other, a decade ago.

Kirk had actually been very good through all that. That was when I still liked Kirk.

All of us helped with Saul's move. Nadia got someone at school to sew the curtains for her—pale green-tinted cream, very nice, with misty gray panels in the center. I scrubbed the place down and bought him a microwave. He was taking a sofa bed and a bookcase out of the apartment, which Kirk and the new boyfriend loaded into the elevator, along with the cartons of Saul's clothes. Ethan, the boyfriend, said, "Good light!" when he entered the room, bowed under the weight of the sofa. He looked different in jeans and a T-shirt, a little stockier.

"I love the light," my brother said. "A new day is dawning here."

He was sitting in a corner while we all worked, and he said, "You know, I really don't need any place bigger."

The new boyfriend looked properly embarrassed. Kirk said, "The couch looks totally great here."

I worried about all this compliance from Saul, this no-problems adaptation to his new situation. Was it sincere? Was it admirable? In my own life, I prided myself on being on good terms with my exes, but I had fought some bitter fights along the way. Nick, Nadia's father, had been so infuriated by what I once said about his personality that he threatened to kidnap Nadia back. Arrive in the night and spirit her away. He didn't mean it—Nadia didn't think so either—but he was hot with anger; he was, as they say, seeing red. What was Saul seeing now? All that talk of light. I wondered if he was seeing a muted glare, if he had a vision of his long days bathed in peaceful beams, streams of brightness in the air all around him. Blessing and bleaching his months in that room, however many months. All that talk of light. He knew more than we did.

And sometimes he slipped into being his former disgruntled self. New York was having a very cold and rainy spring, and when I tried to get him out for a meal of any kind—brunch or dinner or anything—he said, "Who wants to go out in *that?*" Even when the weather had nothing wrong with it, he was annoyed at the prospect of going outside. The bother of it, the inconvenience. And the food. Did I know how greasy the food was in all brunch places? Did I know anything about what he couldn't eat?

Kirk's new boyfriend had not moved in upstairs—he apparently had his own very good apartment on a tree-lined street in the far West Village. I happened to see Kirk in the elevator, and he did not look pleased about anything, but who knew what that meant? "Hey there," I said to him, and he mumbled, "Oh, hello." Not that he could be expected to be overjoyed to see me.

So what did Saul do all day? He looked things up on his computer, he loved antiquarian book sales and knew which prices were rising, he binge-watched TV, he reread some Dickens, he did a little meditating. He kept the place neat and relatively clean, a sign of his fondness for it. And did anyone visit but me?

"Friends come. And people from work. And you know who comes a lot?" he said. "Kirk."

I chuckled bitterly. "Does he help?"

"He brings food. We had strawberries the other day. He says he misses me."

I was fucking tired of the fucking caprices of fucking Kirk. "What do you say?"

"I tell him he has to get used to being alone."

How calm my brother was choosing to be. I hoped it bothered Kirk.

And Saul wasn't rushing to go back to work, was he? He wasn't going back. How had I thought that he would?

"Were you ever in Cambodia?" I asked Saul. "Or was it just Thailand?" I was making tea in his kitchen, the one thing he'd let me do. It was a nice kitchen, blue tiles on the wall.

"Just Thailand. Before I knew Kirk. We went up to the Northeast, not very visited then. Ever go to that part?"

"Not me."

"Great people," Saul said. "Dirt poor. I felt like a jerk as a tourist, with my jangling change. They deserved better."

"Freedom from want," I said. "That was one of the four freedoms in FDR's speech. Nobody thinks of that now as a human right."

"So you want to go to Cambodia?" Saul said. "This is new."

"Remember that guy Bud I used to go with? He lives there."

"I think he treated you not very well," Saul said. "As I remember."

"That was then, this is now," I said.

"Famous last words," Saul said.

Nadia said, "So how did people decide who to marry in the old days when they didn't even sleep together? How did people understand what kind of deal they were getting?"

"Don't ask me," I said. "I didn't come in under that system. But you can't go just by sex, you know. Do I have to tell you that?"

"You so do not," Nadia said, rolling her eyes. "But how

do people make these colossal bargains about what they decide to put up with?"

I knew this wasn't about her own dating life (which was quiet at the moment) but about her friend Kit, set to marry a person whose merits were entirely invisible to Nadia. How to support her friend but not lie too much: that was the problem.

"Lie," I said. I wasn't her parent; I could talk that way to her.

"She thinks he's smart, and he's really stupid. It depresses me what people do."

"You don't know how it will turn out. No one can tell."

"She thinks she's won the lottery," Nadia said. "She feels sorry for the rest of us."

"People are like that," I said. "I used to be like that."

Saul told me he was thinking more about finances lately. He had made a list of how much he spent on rent, how much on food and utilities, what income he had coming in, how much wiggle room he had. He had a little. "I get benefits," he said. "I'm not destitute. I hope you know that."

And, by the way, he'd made a will, and it was in the bookcase by the big book of Audubon drawings, if I wanted to know.

I thought he'd always had a will.

"Well, no. And this one is good. I had someone, a lawyer, make sure everything was all right."

"You found a lawyer without ever leaving the apartment?"

Ethan was a lawyer.

"Estate law isn't his specialty," Saul said, "but I knew he could get the forms for something simple. He made it easy. I just told him what I wanted. Easy as pie."

"How nice."

"Don't forget. By the Audubon book. I stash crucial things there."

I was tearful when Nadia came home. "Saul decided to have a little conversation about his *will*," I said. "What kind of nineteenth-century novel are we in?"

"I hope he doesn't leave all his money to Kirk or anything," she said, after I'd calmed down and she'd poured us a little wine.

I secretly hoped he was leaving whatever he had to Nadia, a person not legally related to either of us.

"He's not rich anyway," she said.

"It doesn't matter," I said.

That was the question about money, wasn't it? How much it mattered. I used to argue with Bud about that, in the old days, when we liked to talk about which friends had good lives. I was always claiming that high incomes soured people and made them stingy and anxious.

"I don't think you should go to Cambodia," Nadia said.

"Who said I was going?"

"Do you know they arrest factory workers if they try to have strikes? It's very unfair."

"I'm not going anywhere anytime soon," I said. I wanted to hop into bed with Bud—that was true, however old we were—but it had nothing to do with the heart of the matter at the moment, which was my brother.

Nadia said, "You mention Bud more than you did."

"Saul knows him. He's not a big fan."

"Excuse me, but Saul is not a proven expert. I wouldn't listen to his opinions about boyfriends if I had any."

"Who would you listen to?"

"Not you either," she said.

What I liked in this was her hopefulness. She was twenty-three, and she was never going to make the mistakes we'd made.

Ethan went with Saul for one of his doctor's visits, on the theory that it was always good to have another person paying attention and writing things down. What kind of world was it, where you needed a lawyer to listen to your doctor?

"He asked good questions," my brother said. "We all had a nice chat. But I don't think I'm going again."

How good could those questions have been? In my opinion, Ethan had been no help at all.

"How can you just not go?" I said.

"A question that answers itself," he said.

I believed in liberty—it was my brother's right not to go anywhere—and it would've done no good if I'd bossed or begged or reasoned. It seemed that the doctor was no longer offering anything he wanted. Saul had more than one doctor, and they were united in their lack of appealing offers.

"It'll be very relaxing," my brother said. "To stay home."

What home? The new place had a good kitchen (better than the old place really), and I believed that if we could keep him eating, he'd have more time. I got this from our mother, always indignant if we didn't finish what was on our plates—"People in other parts of the world would be very happy to eat what you're leaving behind." We were born too late to hear about starving Armenians, but she brought up the people in China (was this about famines under Mao?), and adults were always letting us know that ingratitude about food was dangerous. Did parents in places like Cambodia say this to their children now? Or did the children always eat?

Saul would eat a few things—I could make a very nice corn chowder that he didn't mind and also a Middle Eastern version of fried eggs, with mint, oregano, and scallions. Sometimes he ate pad Thai from a place nearby. On good days he could be tempted by ice cream in certain flavors. He was a slow eater, like a fidgety five-year-old.

On weekends Nadia came with me to deal with the housecleaning. We brought the vacuum cleaner down from Kirk's; in the elevator Nadia wore the hose around her shoulders like a boa. Even with all the dust bunnies collecting under the furniture, the place was so small the work didn't take long, and Saul got to make a joke. "How come," he said, "the Buddhist didn't vacuum in the corners of the room?"

"I know this one," Nadia said.

I didn't. "Because," my brother said, "he had no attachments."

"Oh, my God, she's laughing," Nadia said.

"The woman's been inhaling the floor polish," Saul said.

What did that mean, no attachments? Saul used to tell me it meant *Don't worry, it won't last, nothing does.* And he said all that was more uplifting than it sounded.

"Don't go to Cambodia," Nadia said, when we were eating dinner that night. I was sure I had made it clear to her I wasn't getting on any planes. "How can I deal with stuff that happens with Saul when you're not here? I'm young, you know."

Bud had stopped issuing invitations to Phnom Penh, for lack of an enthusiastic response on my part. Maybe he had found someone else. NGOs were full of intelligent single women. We still had our conversations on Skype. I combed my hair, I put on lipstick; I got excited before he called. We flickered on the screen at each other. That was the way it was.

"I asked Saul," Nadia said, "where he'd want to go if he could get his wish, like they do with kids, that wish foundation. I told him he should go to Jamaica. It's where Kit is going on her ridiculous honeymoon. I'd take him. It's not that far."

"What did he say?"

"He said he liked it fine where he was."

I snorted.

Adults usually didn't act out their wildest wishes before they died, despite all the movies that used that plot. They had other ideas by then. They left the old ones behind.

Nadia started wearing a green ribbon as a choker, in honor of Saul (it looked good on her, she looked good in everything). As a charm, it didn't work. He had a really bad week; he said the bones in his arms and his legs were becoming tunnels of pain. Rats were digging tunnels in his bones all night. By phone I pestered the doctor until he prescribed more painkillers. Maybe not enough—scripts were stingy because of the opioid crisis—but welcome for now. "I'm turning on, tuning in, and dropping out," Saul said. "There's a lot to be said for it."

When we were growing up, there was still some rhetoric left about drugs as a source of enlightenment. When I was in Thailand in my twenties, we could buy anything (or my then-boyfriend could), and we sat around stoned on who knows what. Waiting for moments of strange clarity, which sometimes came. Opiated hash, did people still smoke that? Who came up with that combo?

"Do you remember anything?" Saul said.

"I remember my boyfriend," I said. "Except I've forgotten his name."

Saul laughed. He could still laugh. "Sister Susie," he said.

What did I long for? "Are you discouraged," Bud asked on the screen from Phnom Penh, "because of Trump?"

Yes, but I hadn't remembered to think about it lately. We all had different levels of grief, didn't we, a whole hierarchy.

"In NGOs," Bud said, "the aid workers who see the worst are always going out on the town to get stupidly cheered up. Like those Oxfam Brits who hired prostitutes."

He was my cheering up, a very hygienic form.

"What do you do in Phnom Penh?" I said.

He smirked a little. "Well, there's not much to do. Actually, there is, but I don't do it. There's a bar I like. The girls know me, they don't bother me."

I was glad he wasn't bothered.

"You'd love the river, we have three rivers. And the temples."

"What do Cambodians do for luck?" I was thinking of Nadia and her ribbon.

"Some people get protective tattoos. Angelina Jolie got a Cambodian tattoo."

How far away he was. What did it mean to have a romance that was never going to be acted out? It didn't seem so bad to me anymore. In fact it had certain superiorities over contact in person. And it was as real as the outlines of Angelina Jolie's tattoo (which I'd seen online), with its guardian blessings inked out in Pali. Bud had become a wish of mine with no trouble in it.

Kirk was upset. I could tell by the sight of him, rumpled and frowning, when I ran into him by the recycling bins

in the basement of the building. I was throwing out a bag
of empty cans of ginger ale. It was the one thing Saul liked
now that he was back to not liking again. The cans were
clanging as I dumped them.

"He's not doing well, is he?" Kirk said. "I didn't know
how it would be."

"I guess you didn't," I said.

"Don't be against me," Kirk said.

He wanted me to like him too? I might've pushed him
into the recyclables, if I'd been a different sort of person.
"What's the matter with you?" I said. We seemed to be
connected forever, but so what?

"Did he tell you?" Kirk said. "I asked him to move back."

I gasped out loud, a wheeze of amazement. I had just
been thinking of getting someone to come in a few hours a
day to help, as much as his insurance would cover. Someone good. Not needed now? No longer my business?

"He said no," Kirk said.

"Fuck," I said.

Of course, I was proud of my brother (we don't kneel)
and quite surprised. Kirk had been even more surprised.

"I could help. I'm his friend! He doesn't care," Kirk said.
"He insists that he's happier without me."

Kirk sounded devastated by this bit of news. Which
was probably not even true, though maybe it was. Who
knew what my brother really wanted? He acted now as if

he were in a kingdom whose language was too much work to translate for us.

Kirk was gazing at me, waiting for something he was hoping I could give. "Everybody thinks he's so mild, but he's the stubbornest person on the planet," I said. "No is no."

Kirk said, "Maybe he'll change his mind."

I loved my brother's stubbornness. He didn't have to run around anymore, did he, rushing to get what he thought he should have. Fine where he was. Of course, I envied his freedom, who wouldn't?

Only a few days ago I'd gone into a little fit because I'd lost my favorite earrings; they had been a gift from Nadia's father, whom I didn't even like, but I'd had them for years and they looked good on me. "What are you hanging on to?" Saul said. "You had them and they're gone." This bit of philosophy did stop my wailing. Saul could do that—he could utter a tautology in a way that made it sound beautifully plain and right. "Goodbye to all that," I said to my earrings. Saul was speaking from a spot further on, a better view, speaking with expertise.

Not that he always abided by this. He had spells of being very irritated at me for spending his dollars on overpriced takeout meals or organic detergent—"I'm not made of money." Little pissy amounts of cash. He was afraid of his resources running out. A metaphor there.

Kirk said, "Who knew you would turn into a cheapskate?"

How poorly Kirk understood him; what a mess Kirk had made of everything. Yearning and grabbing. Kirk the now-repentant lummox who dreamed my clearheaded brother would change his mind.

Which he did. Five weeks later, Kirk called to give me the news. "We've got him all settled in." Saul was already in his old bedroom watching TV in a newly rented hospital bed by the time they told me. Kirk paid to rent a bed? Who knew he wanted to be a caretaker? "I'm very comfortable," Saul said. "I have this new kind of pillow under my neck. Ethan got it for me."

"Did they bring up all your stuff? Tell me what you need."

"I think I have everything pretty much."

The one who sounded really, really happy was Kirk. "He looks better already. He does. You can tell by looking at him this is the right move. I never thought he'd say yes. I gave up, I had no clue this would happen. And we got everything done so fast! We did." His voice had gotten giddy and young; he was burbling away.

When I dropped over to see Saul in his new-old lodgings that evening, Kirk was glowing in the doorway. "Ethan made this great little supper that was some kind of mussel stew. And Saul gobbled it up. Well, not all of it, but he ate it. He liked it."

"I ate it in Iceland," Ethan said. "I went there with my mother last year."

Ethan had a mother? I never thought about him outside these rooms. "It's gorgeous," Ethan said about Iceland. "Expensive but worth it." What did a lawyer with a fat paycheck care about expensive?

Kirk said, "Ethan can cook, I can cook. We'll keep trying different food."

"We have a whole bucket of empty mussel shells now," my brother said. My brother with his pinched face, his elbows turned into knobs of bone.

"Ethan's good in the kitchen," Kirk said.

"Now and then I can do something," Ethan said. "But you know how late I work."

"I can't eat late," Saul said. "Don't expect me to stay up. I get tired."

"He ate ice cream too," Kirk had to tell me.

Whatever the report of his chef's skills, Ethan slipped out soon after I arrived. There was murmuring with Kirk by the door, and he was gone.

"Hey," my brother said, when Kirk walked back in, "I don't have to do the dishes now, do I?"

Kirk acted as if that were the funniest thing he'd ever heard. "We just throw them out when they're dirty," he said. Did I actually laugh too?

Soon after, the two of us walked my brother to his old room. Saul showed me the way a person could crank the bed down to make it easy to climb into. "A miracle of science," he said. "It's costing a fortune, I think."

"Good night, sweet prince," Kirk said.

On the way back, I saw from the hallway that Kirk's usually pristine computer studio was a mess, with piles of clothes littering it. It had become the room where he slept. (Alone, it seemed. Not with Ethan at the moment.)

"He's crazy about that bed," Kirk said. "Did you see that? He is."

When the sunlight, which my brother used to love, bothered his eyes, even in this dimmer apartment, Ethan set up curtains around the bed. He had someone construct posts at the bed's four corners, and then he hung the elegant drapes that Nadia had designed—they became bed curtains, like the ones Scrooge had around his bed when the ghosts frightened him.

Nadia still thought the curtains looked good, the pale green on the sides and misty gray on the top and bottom. She was not a fan of Kirk ("why do I have to like him?"), but she made an effort when I took her to visit. We were all sitting around the living room, and Ethan brought in tea and a plate of pastel meringue kisses from a bakery, a light delicacy for Saul. "How pretty they are," Nadia said.

Kirk said, "The tea looks too strong. Saul needs it weaker. Can you bring in the hot water?"

"You know nothing about tea," Ethan said, but he was back with the kettle in a jiffy. "Taste it," he said to my brother.

"Just right," Saul said.

"You're sure?" What attention Saul was getting, what tender fuss. I could see him basking in it.

He was chomping and sipping, king of the table. Between bites he said, "We watched this thing on TV that was really hilarious."

"We were totally into it," Ethan said.

"I couldn't stop laughing in one part," Kirk said.

Nadia got all the details (a Tig Notaro appearance), and my brother imitated her deadpan style. Kirk cracked up watching him. "You missed your calling in stand-up," he said.

"He went for the big bucks in library science," Ethan said.

Saul couldn't resist telling how he'd once spilled an entire cartload of books on a library trustee, a story I'd heard many times before. As had Kirk. My brother told it well this time. Nadia laughed at the oafish amazement of the fallen trustee, Saul's version of his own loony apologies, but the one who loved the tale the most was Kirk. He gazed and nodded at my brother; he clapped and hooted. I'd rarely seen him so happy.

Saul, for his part, had the sly look people get when they've told a joke that's gone over. How pleased my brother was, on that pinched face of his.

When we left, Nadia muttered to me in the elevator, "So I guess he's okay there." Her face was still tinted pink from laughing, but now her voice was flat. The whole thing had confused her about the nature of love. I wasn't saying a word either. What did I know? I was thinking that this would become an elemental part of what she'd remember, for who knew how long, that she'd have what she'd just seen. The way they were, just like that—I wanted her to have that.

5 / Bud

My father, who meant well about some things and not about others, died at seventy, not that old. He'd been living in our house in New Jersey, with caretakers around him, and in the front window was a bumper sticker that said, *Get US Out! of the United Nations.* He'd once been a member of the very-far-right John Birch Society and maybe always was (we didn't keep in close touch). In our years together, when the Cold War was still on, my father took pride in never being duped by the insidious plots of those trying to turn the U.S. into a socialist hell, a pride that rode on urgency. Every day he woke up to important work. The sticker in the window did not look that old, actually.

My mother was now long since married to someone else, but my sister and my brother lived nearby. How green and hilly the countryside looked, how pretty these older suburbs seemed. The maple trees in the front of our house had grown into vast leafy giants. I'd flown in from another continent, and when they saw me my sibs said, "Oh! You're here!" as if they hadn't believed my voice on the phone. We were gathered on the front porch.

I was glad enough to see them. Cecie, my sister, was looking a little dried out but not bad, and my brother, Dillon, was portly in a friendly way. "This is it," Cecie said, which meant she was really very sad.

"It *is* it," I said. He was my father. I had my sadness too.

"He had the life he wanted," my brother said. That was enough; we didn't need to go any deeper into it.

I was the youngest, and my parents' marriage was already in trouble by the time I appeared, so my father neglected me a little, which was a good thing. I knew from what he said at dinner that a dangerous New World Order was being planned by people who might seem nice. It was 1961 when I started first grade, and the Iron Curtain was still down. I was too shy to be a pain in elementary school, but I must've uttered these opinions enough that people knew what I was.

My one friend was a boy named Will—we were Will and Bill—whose parents were in the thing too. We were obsessed with cars, both of us, and all we wanted to do was play with all the toy ones we had, race them, make champions of them; sometimes we gave them names and had stories for them. We went through a phase of constructing model ones too, a hundred plastic parts to be glued and painted. We were little pedants of the auto industry; we knew a lot. I had a dream that someday I'd drive a car in a secret army that shot at the hidden Communist enemies of my country; I'd fire with deadly aim and speed away.

Before seventh grade Will's family decided to move to California. We said we would write but we didn't. I had no other friends, and I was suddenly lonely in a way I hadn't been before—the nights were the worst—and that was when I became a reader. Technically, I was only allowed certain kinds of books, but it wasn't that hard to smuggle things into my room. The maid did the cleaning, and my taste in literature was nothing to her. I had a library card; my prep school made us each get one. I loved any murder mystery, however old or young the level of it was, and I loved Dickens, which they might have thought was harmless anyway.

In seventh grade a cute girl in my English class named Sally asked me what kind of music I liked. I said Easy Listening. It was already well into the sixties, and neither of my parents allowed what they called jungle music in the house. Sally started me on Motown—the Temptations, the Supremes, Martha and the Vandellas. I was so pleased to be invited into her living room, listening to her records on the family hi-fi, that I told her the stuff was pretty good. Of course, I had heard some of it before, blasting out the windows of people's cars, through the sound systems in clothing stores, but I hadn't much listened, and what I heard now was the throbbing sorrow—*Baby, baby, baby, don't leave me*—and a surprising strength in the wailing about it. My family hated weakness, but this was a whole other form of complaint.

Sally's mother, who didn't know me from Adam, liked me because I had such a short haircut, and she brought us Cokes and salted peanuts. I knew I was turning a corner, chomping down the snacks, slurping from a straw, tapping the rhythms on my knee, in this alien house, and I even thought for a second that I might slyly bring them over to better thinking about the world. I hardly spoke at that age, so how could I have done this? Sally had lots more to play for me, if I didn't need to go home yet. My father said then and later that females were my undoing.

Not that it happened all at once. As much as I loved being at Sally's, as stunned as I was that she liked me, I felt weird and monstrous once I walked through the door of my own house. Nor could I keep this feeling to myself. I told my parents (who were in the living room, sipping highballs before dinner) that I couldn't stand this crazy, silly rock 'n' roll Sally had played for me. My parents did not immediately ban her from my acquaintance—that came later—but it started my father on a rant about how the lowest elements in the population were ruining our culture. I was scared of my father sometimes, but my mother's increasing quarrels with him had taken away my awe. "The songs weren't *that* bad," I said. My father slammed the coffee table with his hand.

"What's the matter with you?" he said. It wasn't the last time he said it either.

The Birchers were already in decline—though my parents would not have admitted it—and even my brother and sister strayed a little, in time. But I had the worst of it with my family; I horrified them the most, with good reason. At first I just wanted to be a modified form of them, a hip and witty sort of Young Republican. Which they would have despised too. I tried not arguing, but teenagers are not good at that. When my fulminating father ordered me to my room right now right this minute, I went. I'd mutter things like, "America is rank with injustice," which made my mother shriek and made my father actually kick me once, hard and sharp, in the shin—a terrifying moment, what if he didn't stop?—and I went straight to my room until released. That degree of obedience faded as I got older.

I ran away for the first time when I was fifteen. I wasn't

wild or street-smart, and I thought I would go stay with my brother, who was in a super-conservative college north of Pittsburgh. I called him from a phone booth when I got to Port Authority, and he said, "You have to go back, Billy boy, I'm sorry."

The waiting room was full of benches and I sat on one, which meant that a nutty bag lady started asking me to drive her to Alaska. When I moved, a guy half-asleep decided to rest his head on my shoulder and his hand on my thigh. I was already six one, bigger than he was, but fear was in me when I shook him off. "Hey!" he said. I moved my seat to the other side, and then I woke to a police officer gripping my shoulder. "Time to go," he said.

Later I made this a story for Sally. I said the cop had been a voice from on high, words from a cloud. I'd been in a daze of stubborn blank, deserted by my wits, defeated. I got up and found the last bus of the night back to our part of New Jersey and walked the four miles from the final stop to our house. My parents were waiting. "What do you think you're doing?" my mother said. My glamorous mother looked witchy and shrewish, a skinny angry woman in a bathrobe.

"There's something wrong with you," my father said.

After this I had stricter curfews and my room was searched. After this there was talk of exiling me to an uncle in Tennessee (never happened). After this I started smoking dope with Sally. I was different after this even though it had been a mess. (I would say that about a number of things in my life, actually.) I had lunged into the outside world, and although there had been plenty to alarm and dishearten me, I had survived—I was fine—a sensation so interesting it became addictive.

Even Sally was afraid I was never going to finish high school because I ran away so many times. I discovered hitchhiking—I'd walk to the next town (I was a great walker) and stick out my thumb. Once I got all the way to Philadelphia, where I panhandled money for lunch and slept in a park near a museum. Once I got to a campground in another part of the state and made a mattress out of my jacket. Once I went to Manhattan and just walked all night, sticking to streets where stores were still lit. I was an amateur as a runaway—two days were my maximum—and I never joined the clans crashing in apartments or lazing in encampments on city streets. When I was home, I even did schoolwork. But I hardly talked to my parents. My father called me a deluded hoodlum and raged when I wouldn't answer him. He'd say, "Wake up!" and chop at the back of my neck with his hand. My mother, who could be very icy, would say, "You used to have a brain." At night I'd slip out my window—I was a good climber, I knew where the ledges were—and sneak up into Sally's house, which I had to leave before dawn.

"Ah, look what's flown in," Sally would say. That was the one piece of luck in my situation. Girls liked me. It was probably my aloofness, but there was also something in my looks. Sally had another boyfriend by then, but she never turned me away. And I could feel the gazes of young women on me when I was walking in new places. I wasn't exactly at ease with new people, but girls did the work of talking to me.

I managed to graduate from my stuffy prep school; I'd been there enough days, and they gave up on me. I hadn't applied to any colleges—I'd always thought I'd have to, or else be drafted, but the war wound down and the draft ended, just in time for me. My parents thought I should work for a year to give me a chance to mature, and I had spoken to one of their friends about a future in retail management, whatever that was. Of course, the night after graduation I was gone, escaped on a train with a duffle full of books and sweaters and underwear.

I had someone waiting for me. When I got off at the Hoboken station, almost deserted at one a.m., there she was by the closed newsstand—my lovely Lizzie, with her long dark hair and her pale eyes, the agent of my future. She was twenty years old and she had an apartment she shared with two roommates in New Brunswick, where she was going to college. She was the best friend of Sally's sister, and I had met her at a birthday picnic. I was good at picking up girls by then.

What an astounding sight she was, in the Hoboken waiting room. I drew her to me, gave her a long kiss. We were high on the drama of it. The station was dingy and cavernous, paint peeled from its very walls, and we were in a great scene in the tale of something important and we knew it.

She had her car outside, a heavily dented Dodge Dart, and I drove it—I always drove—and I knew the way too. It was a warm, rainy night. We hardly spoke (I liked that she wasn't gabby) except when I said, "I love this weather," and she chuckled.

Dale and Betsy, her roommates, were still up and had a little reception for us when we arrived. They had cheap wine; they had a box of Entenmann's chocolate chip cookies. "Live free or die," they toasted. Everybody liked my story—right-wing demons spawn normal child—and my flight had already become a legend they lived with.

It was not the first night I'd spent in Lizzie's bed, and we were sleepy and drunk by the time we started in, but we were bold creatures, it was our night to be bold. "Hey," she said, when we were done, "there's something in this, isn't there?"

The next day I phoned my parents from a pay phone

in a drugstore. My mother said, "Hello," and I said, "Don't worry, I'm fine," and hung up. Did I really think they could trace the call? How many detective shows had I seen? When I walked out to the lunch counter and ate a hot dog with Lizzie, I was still concentrating on my mother's voice, familiar all my life and now lost. Love or no love, I had more than loosened the ties; I had torn them. I had stopped being their son, and later they would say just that.

I looked like any of my friends (less shaggy maybe), but I lived in a different stage of life, inside an older person's fate. I had left home. Why hadn't I known how indelible this would be? I had a little practice, from running away in brief spurts, but not enough; I could see it wasn't enough. Lizzie, who was nobody's fool, said, "It went okay?"

"Not bad," I said. "Short."

We had the day to celebrate, which meant dashing home to go back to bed. But the next day was Monday and Lizzie was starting her summer job at a day camp, tending a band of seven-year-olds. Betsy was filing records in the admissions office; Dale was taking linguistics in summer school; I had the place to myself. I smoked what was left of somebody's stash, but I saw the problem at once. My time had no purpose and I had no money; I was on the edge of a void deeper and wider than I was ready for.

By dinner I had what could pass for a theory. Didn't a town like New Brunswick need cab drivers? I loved cars; I knew more about them than most people. The next day I was told you had to be twenty-one to get a hack license in the state. Couldn't I lie? I tried, with another company. "I could have you fucking arrested, bud," the fleet owner said. One thing I didn't want was my parents getting any phone calls.

I gave Dale twenty hand-written cardboard signs to put up around campus: *cheap rides offered, no distance too short or too far*. I had to clean up Lizzie's car, and I had to stay home by the phone, and the name on the ads was Bud the World's Best Chauffeur (to throw my parents off the track, not that they were on any track). For days the phone never rang. The first call was a weeping sophomore who'd cut her hand with a cheese knife and wanted a trip to the emergency room. I got her there fast, and I waited and drove her back to her dorm.

This was the beginning of my great rep as a driver. I could be called at any time of night, I would go anywhere, and I watched out for the safety of female passengers. (It was not a safe era—walkers on city streets were held up at knifepoint; Patty Hearst had gotten kidnapped without even leaving her apartment.) Lizzie had not meant to surrender her car, and she was also concerned, not wrongly, about all those lively young women getting into it.

I was proud of this job I'd invented, the little bits of cash that kept coming in. I was doing well, for me. Every few weeks I called my parents and left a fast message. Once I heard my mother say, "Oh, Billy," and I asked how she was. "What do you care?" she said. It was a real question, under the biting sarcasm. I'd forgotten she once liked me. And I'd thought it was so nice of me to call.

"You always take the best view of yourself," Lizzie said.

Maybe so. I had my arrogance. And I had missed my parents but not in the way other kids might; I knew I lived without the same habits of feeling most people had. What could I ever say? *Yes she's my mother but.* Who'd want to be me?

Lizzie trotted out my history when people visited. My parents believed the civil rights movement was all about setting up a Negro-Soviet republic. They thought that public water fluoridation was part of a conspiracy to poison the nation. I was used to all of it, but our friends shrieked. And it made me sound special and interesting, which we both thought I was. She had taken me on, dear Lizzie. I never wanted to thank her out loud but I was intensely grateful. And I was more playful with her than I had been with anyone. We had games, we had jokes, we had forms of glee.

I stayed with Lizzie for two years. I grew up with her. The thing was over when she found out that her roommate Dale had beckoned me into her room more than once, on certain afternoons. I had not taken Dale that seriously but I certainly hadn't turned her away. Nor did I really think there was anything wrong with it (people did everything), but I knew how Lizzie would think.

I had never paid rent, and I had enough money to buy a rattletrap car, a once-white Volkswagen Beetle. I took off and by not letting it overheat on steep hills, I got myself to Vermont without stalling out once. I was lonely for Lizzie and I sent her postcards—"Miss you, babe" and "Wish you were with me"—that she had no way to answer. I had never lived in the country but I somehow thought it would do me good—starry skies, endless horizons—and I read a listing on a bulletin board in a supermarket for a cheap room to rent. The room was in a group house, so at least I had people.

Everybody in the house had to work in the local food co-op—that was how we got food for cheap—and I was okay about throwing potatoes into bags or sweeping floors, but I was always late. The guy who was the director said, "Assholes like you think you don't have to do anything," and a woman named Eileen took pity on me. "He's such a show-off," she said, "and you're not." Flirting with her got me the job of driving the delivery truck—she was on a committee—and this turned into a semi-paying job when they needed more hours.

Did I like living in the country? I did in the summer

and fall—Eileen took me to the prettiest lake for swimming and to the mountain with the reddest maples. She tended to be more needy and pesty than Lizzie had ever been but I didn't care at first. Oh, I hated the winter. The house was underheated for economy and I walked around like a zombie in long underwear and thick sweaters. And then we got robbed.

The whole house had gone off to a Christmas shindig for the co-op. When we got home the door was swinging open, and behind it sofa cushions were thrown on the floor. In our rooms, drawers were yanked out of dressers. We weren't a very affluent group, but they'd ripped a stereo out of the wall and Eileen lost a pearl necklace from her mother. Something violent had stormed through the house—they had moved with speed and roughness, spilling and wrenching and dumping.

"Why did they come *here?*" Eileen said. "Do they hate us?"

"It was somebody poor," one of the guys said. "People rob out of necessity."

They'd taken a hundred dollars from my underwear drawer, which infuriated me and made me want to punch the guy who talked about necessity. Though I thought he was probably right. I felt naive and corrected, as many of us did. Danger was all around us, always had been, like the mice in the walls we could hear at night.

It was an era with lawlessness all over (friends of Lizzie's used to get mugged on campus). In truth I had stolen a few things myself—a pair of work gloves from the feed store in town, a quilted vest from the Army-Navy store. Nothing from anyone I knew.

Christmas Day in the house was full of bitter talk—about the robbers who despised us and might come back again— though one of the men said, "Easy come, easy go. It's a mistake to care about *things*. It's a lesson."

"Who wants that fucking education?" someone said.

I sort of liked being independent of possessions, if you were going to talk about it that way. I wasn't vain about having stuff. On the other hand, winter made me wolfish. I would've fought hard for my coverings if anyone had reached for them.

"What do the poor have to do," Eileen's best friend said, "to qualify as miserable?"

"They have government agencies deciding just that," her boyfriend said.

Our budget Christmas dinner was turkey wings with gravy—not bad—and as I gnawed I said, "My father would've said people make their own poverty by being lazy." My parents had trouble imagining other people.

Someone said this was too depressing for Christmas,

and we got into appropriate talk about whose relative made the worst fruitcakes.

The robbery made me feel differently about money. It made me think of it as impermanent. I'd been so proud of my little hoard of bills and poof they were gone. My goal in life just then was to take care of myself without being bound by the usual strictures; like my parents, I believed in freedom. I was going to have to do better than this.

It snowed three days straight right after New Year's. Beautiful, but the chains on the tires were a joke and the heater in the truck barely worked. What was I doing in this godforsaken part of the country? I wanted out. Eileen howled when I said this—she had a different concept of us than I did. I was too fucking broke to go anywhere. It was a long winter, and in early March the house cat Freddie got himself up a maple tree and for three days he didn't come down. I had to climb almost to the top to get him down, and I did it barehanded in the cold, to keep my grip. "You should be a cat burglar," one of the women said.

I thanked her for the career advice. I was a self-taught climber, but I had talent, which, like all my attributes, was wasted here. Too bad there wasn't any tall building with cash in it anywhere in the town. Well, there was a nice restaurant in the next town, built in what had been someone's idea of a castle. Provincial show-offs went there to eat chanterelles. It had so many ledges and niches it wouldn't be hard to climb, if you knew what you were doing. On a Sunday morning in May, a cook coming in to set up brunch discovered there had been a break-in through an upper story, and someone had made off with the Friday and Saturday proceeds.

What I thought, as I was crawling over that roof, was *This shit-brain idea is going to kill me, I'm going to break like a bottle when I fall.* I had to keep telling myself to keep moving ahead, not to think. But when I twisted through the turret window, which wasn't even locked, and actually found the cash box in a drawer in the attic office, I was so proud I had to keep from roaring. It was a great moment for me.

The next day I took the box far into the woods to split the lock open and count the returns—$613. A lovely sight. And if any house residents thought it was me, they didn't say so. Bragging was a temptation—I heard myself say, "Very athletic burglary," but Eileen wasn't that quick on the uptake. I picked a fight with her about whether paper garbage bags were bad for the planet, and two days later I left for Boston.

I might've had more of a future as a criminal—I liked it—but I lacked companions in the life. In Boston I got myself a room at a Y on Huntington Avenue, and among the very mixed group of residents it was my luck to fall in with the nerdy young dropouts. A scuzzy but harmless group, and we celebrated my twenty-first birthday drinking cheap beer and discussing the future of the American empire. We were all glad that it looked doomed.

I did two other things on my birthday: I applied for a hack license and I called my parents. Who had no rights over me now, if they ever had. "What's the news?" I said. My mother was so confused she was silent at first.

There was news. My sister Cecie was engaged to a guy they liked; my brother was not doing well in law school. Also my parents were talking about getting a divorce, but I didn't learn that till later. My mother said, "We almost forgot all about you."

My mother had a spiteful tongue when offended. I didn't blame her, though I once had. They had become less real to me, all of them, and maybe I had to them. We were like Israelis and Palestinians who'd once lived in the same valley but now were on opposite sides. Nobody had forgotten anything.

I got hired by a guy with a fleet of cabs, and although Boston was an especially insane city to drive in, I liked my job. I met all sorts of people, especially girls. Two friends from the Y found an apartment near Fenway Park and I made enough money to share the place with them. The other thing about Boston was that everybody was sort of in school in some way, picking up a course or starting again. I heard schools looked fondly on nontraditional students, which I'd certainly be if I ever went back.

I brought a girl to my sister's wedding. The invitation had come to my apartment, my parents requesting the pleasure of my company at the wedding of their daughter Cecilia Susan. I bought a suit at Goodwill and talked Phoebe into a trip to New Jersey in my car. I'd met her when I drove her home from a bar, a tiny pretty brunette, drunk out of her mind, amused by all the ads on signs along the way; her own address was a riot to her. We were enjoying the ridiculousness of the world together, and I did what I wasn't supposed to, I went upstairs to her apartment when she asked. We were both jubilant—I tried not to rush but I did—and I had to rise from that bed to finish my night shift. She said, "Yeah, yeah, I know." I called the next day, worried she hated me now, but she said, "Hey! It's you!" and turned out to be a serious, friendly person when sober. She worked for a poor-kids charity, writing their appeals. And she was instantly a fan of my favorite diner, she thought their French toast was perfect, she liked anything I wanted to do. I didn't think she was going to stay with someone like me—a woman who got up to go to an office every day—but we definitely had a thing.

For my sister's wedding, she wore a dress that was a patchwork of vintage silk prints, quite hip at the time, and she had put a fake gardenia in her hair. But we got there a little late (my fault) and edged into the back of the church with half the service over. My sister—there she was!—was marrying a guy who didn't look that bad. Under her filmy veil, she was pink in the face from the big deal of it all.

"After three years away, you couldn't even get here on time?" my father said to me at the reception. He was a little stouter, a little older.

"Thanks, Dad, you look great too," I said.

"I guess you heard I'm an ogre," he said, when he shook Phoebe's hand. She chuckled politely.

My mother was better. She leaned up to hug me, flooding me with her carnation perfume, and said, "So, so glad you're here." She looked good, the smiling mom of the bride. And my sister cried when I kissed her; my brother clapped me on the back a long time. I was just getting sentimental, also a little drunk, when my father gave his toast, which had the phrase "nation of families" in every clause.

"Mom's leaving, you know," my brother said. "It's our last time all together."

"Not Dad's idea, I'm sure."

"He broke the windows in her car when she told him."

I thought about my father's fury and the little he ever got from it. He roared and raged and grabbed with all his might at what couldn't be held on to. His pretty wife, his youngest son, the crazy oligarchical America in his head— gone, gone, phantoms in the mist. How futile all that grasping was. Not that I felt sorry for him.

My brother said, "Cute girl you brought."

Phoebe, who'd had even more champagne than I had, said, "Why do people spend all this money on weddings? Children are starving all over the country. No one here believes that, do they?"

I lost track of her, while my brother and I were reminiscing about playing Foosball, and she went over to the caterers who were hauling away the platters and explained to them where they could donate the leftovers (in Boston, four hours away). My mother was right near her and said, "It would just be a mess."

By the time I got there, Phoebe was telling her she had no idea what a mess was. And a few other things. "Your mother has been having a lovely day," my father informed me. "I think you will have to remove your guest from the premises."

Phoebe was not even shouting, not really, just discussing cases of mothers feeding toddlers out of garbage bins. I myself had been gladly scarfing down the oysters Rockefeller, the filet mignon, the potatoes dauphinoise—when did I get to eat anything like that? I was disappointed to be sent off before they cut the wedding cake, with its tiers of buttercream flowers, and I considered (just for a second) having Phoebe wait in the car, she could read a book. But we left together, and I said to my sister, "Great party, have a great honeymoon."

I was too drunk to drive and so was Phoebe (we knew that much), so I parked two blocks away from the banquet hall and we slept in the Beetle. I woke in the darkest hour of the night, too tall to be curled in that seat, not happy with Phoebe. They weren't her family; she had no right. Though no one had made me bring her. I had a surge of disdain for all of us at the wedding, the entire human cluster of us, muttering and pretending and blaring our opinions; I thought the whole notion of families was misguided and false.

I wouldn't let Phoebe apologize either, when she woke up and felt bad. "I could send them a letter," she said. "Give me the address, I can write."

"Leave it," I said. "Don't make it worse."

I wasn't going back. The episode, which had not been their fault, made me want to stay away from the whole mess of it, far as I could. To keep on as I was, apart from them. But what did I think then—that I could be a person without what are called ties of blood? I did think that. And I could be, as it turned out; I made my way like that. It made no sense in most parts of the world. No parents, no wife, no children? People all over the planet were amazed.

On the way home with Phoebe, I said she'd been right to yell about how no one cared how many children were starving in America. But then we had an argument about the royal family of Britain. I made a crack about an aunt of mine acting like the Duchess of Windsor, and Phoebe said the duchess had been a Nazi, and I said, "I don't think so."

"You think I can't ever, ever know anything," Phoebe said.

What did I care? It was like the fights people have in bars, where they get violent over half-known facts. We squabbled and sniped until we stopped for coffee off the highway. "Look it up," she said, and then we ordered chocolate donuts and tried to remember we liked each other. In fact we were never the same as a couple.

I had to go to the library a few days later to read in the *Encyclopedia Britannica* that the duke and duchess had visited prewar Germany and much admired Hitler. (Okay, it didn't say they were party members.) Why had I scoffed? Phoebe had accused me of having the overconfidence of the elite. Cause of all the evil in the world.

And then I found myself reading around in that volume (*W* for *Windsor*) of the *Britannica*, a reference source my

parents had always condemned. *Wallaby; warbler; Welling-
ton, Duke of; Wright, Orville and Wilbur.* I got lost in the
pages all morning. I came home and told my roommates
that the Battle of Waterloo was really very nearly won by
Napoleon's side. I was so pleased to know this.

And that was how I talked myself into going back to
school. In fact, school was nothing like that. It was all
about writing papers and arguing theories, about naming
concepts and identifying principles. I took poli sci and eco-
nomics and even some physics. UMass had fees but I could
pay them in pieces. It took me six years to finish. Trudy,
my girlfriend at the end, was a bartender, and she brought
home a bottle of Jack Daniel's to celebrate. "What a lot of
bullshit a degree is," I said, knocking back a shot, but I had
my pride in the thing. I wrote to my mother (I could do
that) and my brother and my sister to tell them. My sister
had two kids by then, not that I'd much noticed.

I was still driving a cab. I'd gotten held up by a guy with
a pistol once, in the early years, and I'd had my share of
raving passengers, but I might've kept at it forever. I liked
it fine. Out of the blue, my sister wrote to say she and her
husband were coming to Boston for something, would I
have lunch with them?

I wrote back yes.

Trudy made fun of me as I got cleaned up to go. (I was definitely not taking any girlfriends this time.) I shaved with care, slicked down my hair, put on a decent sweater. "Mr. Power Elite," she said.

"Nations tremble," I said.

I was supposed to meet them in the restaurant of their hotel, which meant mediocre food, but what did I care? What I didn't realize until I walked into the room was that they had their kids with them. A little guy in a sailor cap was sitting in a high chair next to Cecie, and Cecie, plumper now, was putting a spoon in his mouth. She leaned up to kiss me and said, "Dad doesn't even want me to talk to you."

Her husband, whose name I had forgotten, said, "But we're extremely glad to see you. Thanks for coming out."

I shook hands with the older boy, who was maybe four, a gesture that amused him highly. I waved to the baby.

"Dad's still mad about the wedding," my sister said. "He thinks you and your lady friend were trying to organize all the workers."

"We should have," I said.

"Let's not go there," my sister said.

I made funny faces for the kids, and I asked how Mom was doing.

"I never knew she was so miserable before," my sister said. "She said this is the first happiness she's known.

The new husband is a goon who drinks too much, but she likes him."

"I hope he has money," I said.

"Dad has a rule about not mentioning your name," my sister said. "He thinks you stole Dillon's hi-fi. The night you left."

This was a bit of an exaggeration. How could I have run off on the train with two mahogany-encased speakers and an amp and a turntable? I had only taken Dillon's portable cassette recorder, a plastic box the size of a hardback novel, which he never used anyway.

"He holds that against me?" I said. "It was eight years ago."

"Brother stealing from brother," she said. "That and the union thing at the wedding."

"So what are you up to these days?" her husband said.

I said that I had a job at the headquarters of Local 1199 of the National Union of Hospital and Health Care Employees. I was at a desk most of the day—answering phone calls, trying to get hold of people, getting flyers printed— but I enjoyed the work. It was Norm, one of my old roommates, who actually held this job, but he would not have minded my seizing it for the purpose at hand.

"We'll keep that under our hats," my sister said. "If you don't mind."

"What the fuck do I care?" I said.

"Little pitchers," my sister said.

I asked the older boy if he liked Bert and Ernie, and we had a brief discussion of Muppet plots (which Trudy and I liked to watch when we were stoned). I got to be his uncle for maybe twenty minutes, and I did an excellent imitation of Miss Piggy—"Are you looking at *moi?*"—which he liked. When the baby started to fuss, we all said our goodbyes.

So that was how I started my career with Local 1199. I told Norm I wanted a job there if he ever heard of anything, and it took months, but he found me a spot. It meant a pay cut, but by then I was fixed on it as my destiny. I did more running around than what I'd told my sister—there was always a drive where I was handing out pamphlets outside a hospital. Plenty of people on the street ignored us. Reagan had fired the striking air controllers the year before, so it was not a cheerful time for unions. This made us cozy with each other. I dated quite a few nurses.

I followed one of them to New York. It was the summer I turned thirty-three—Angelica, my girlfriend, got a gig at St. Vincent's, right in the Village, and I managed a transfer to 1199's big central office. I went around saying I loved this city, a statement that surprised some, since a flaming desperation ran through certain districts, certain parks, at the time, and its name was crack. Used vials glinted in the gutters, and the rest of the city went on being stylish. Angelica was a tough bird, but ravaged addicts made her hard job harder, and she sort of hated my being so upbeat. "Do you *like*," she said, "being in a place where the worst is happening?"

"Not when you put it that way," I said. "But I do."

I had been brought up to despise chaos, which probably gave me an affection for lots of the chaos I met. I was not too old to have actually tried crack (just twice), and I'd liked it fine—I liked the insidious brain-lift of it, all too brief. Drug use in the mid-eighties involved a certain reckless hope that wasn't entirely alien to me. "People have a right to fuck up," I said.

She groaned. And yet Angelica and I got along very well. She was a practical person, a fan of evidence before theory, much less opinionated than anyone I knew. The hospital had put her on night shift for now—our schedules did not synch—and that may have helped us live together. Sometimes I got out of bed in the early morning to greet her, fed us both dishes of ice cream, before we slipped back into bed.

One December she took me home to meet her family in the Philippines, in a town outside Manila. The family wasn't crazy about me, but I loved that part of the world at once. I couldn't get over the palms, the ferns, the hibiscus, the heat, the haze, the ambling pace. I was in another time zone of history. (Angelica said I was attracted to under-development.) Even Manila had beauty around the edges of its streets. How could I, with my Anglo genes, be such a tropical creature? But I was. I took off for a few days without Angelica and did some hiking in the highlands. It beat Vermont by a mile, in my opinion.

Angelica was glad I liked it there but she was suspicious of my getting so carried away about it. Did I not care about the lack of a living wage for those charming locals in their adorable shacks? Or did I forget that on vacation? During the plane ride home, we suddenly seemed to be on different sides of experience. Her family had probably put pressure on her. Angelica herself was looking to marry, sometime in the approximate future, and I was not up for marrying anyone. She knew that.

We didn't last all that much longer after the trip. She would fall into fits of ill temper against me, as if I had betrayed her by being who I was. "You can't get away with this forever," she said. It was a harder breakup than I expected.

But after that I was a travel addict, always trying to get myself to somewhere in Southeast Asia, that leafy tangle of uneven development between India and Australia. I knew where to get cheap flights, I piled up sick days to wangle longer vacations, I got by on very little when I was there. I liked wherever I went—Malaysia, Thailand, Sumatra, Java—year after year. The guys at the union called me Jungle Rat.

There was a rumor at the union office that I came from a family with mansions in these places, that I had a trust fund I kept under wraps. I had freely admitted to someone that my father owned a company that made paper boxes for other companies. Trudy used to say she could tell a certain kind of private school from my speech, though my speech had changed. Were you always and forever what you were born into? I had set up my life relying on other principles.

My mother used to say, when I called her, "Do you remember anything about us at all?" My mother's new husband—he wasn't even so new anymore—had moved them to a fancy retirement community, which she actually liked.

In fact, I had forgotten a lot. I went for so long without talking about much of it. And none of it was the same now anyway. I'd made a few visits. We all looked different now.

"I guess you're the black sheep," one of the guys at work said.

"I'm the goat," I said. "I'm the wild pig."

People think you'll always go back someday, that home is what you are and it'll claim you. But I was on a different system. It wasn't for everyone, but I liked my system.

✦ ✦ ✦

I was in Isan, in the Northeast of Thailand, where I'd been having a great time riding a motorcycle along a lake with pink water lilies, when the bad news about my father reached me. From a pay phone in a post office in Udon Thani, I made a call to my phone machine to check my messages and I heard Cecie's voice, starting slow—"I'm just calling to say"—with the soberly worded sentence that our father had passed away. From a cancer he'd apparently had for a while, which she thought I knew about but I didn't. The message was only two days old.

"Just get on a plane," Cecie said, when I called her. "You can do that. Just get here."

It cost a lot to change the ticket, and all through the long multi-stop plane ride I naturally thought, *Why do I think I have to show up for any of this?* I missed the funeral itself, as it happened. I was in the sky somewhere over the Pacific when they were saying the words. Whatever was said. He had friends but not many; he picked fights with them. Nothing was more irresistible to him than a flash of indignation. I was seeing him at the dinner table, his snickers and growls and bouts of high dudgeon at whatever the news was; I was hearing his voice, all through the sleepless hours when I leaned back with my eyes closed, in that undersized seat on the plane.

I called Cecie from a pay phone at the airport. It was ten at night, New York time.

"Well," Cecie said. "Here you are. Good to hear your voice. Come tomorrow. There are legal matters. Dillon wants to see you too."

"Not too early, okay?"

"Come to the house," she said. "You know where the house is."

I'd been away from the house itself for two decades. Of course, I'd seen it in dreams.

"How are the kids?" I asked Cecie, while we stood on the porch.

"Well, you know. They're upset. Charlie's thirteen already. And Laird's in fifth grade."

"Smart as whips," Dillon said.

Cecie was fooling with a key to the front door. "Place should maybe have a coat of paint on it before we sell it," she said.

An oxygen tank had been wheeled into the foyer, probably waiting to be picked up. Inside, the old beige sofa was now a charcoal color, and the rugs were gone. The house was a spooky structure, empty and mean.

"I wanted you to have a little time here," Cecie said, "because the will says we're entitled to select whatever things we want. I was going to take the glass coffee table, if nobody minds."

"I don't mind."

"Walk around if you want to," Cecie said. "There isn't any formal reading of the will. They only do that in the movies."

"Want to hear what it says?" Dillon asked.

I wasn't sure I did, but they started in. Ninety percent of my father's assets was to be split equally between Cecie and Dillon, and the remaining ten percent was assigned to me. With certain conditions.

"No," I said. "What?"

"It's left to you in a trust," Cecie said, "with executors, who are us. You get interest payments. And there's a clause that says you lose it all if you make an unsuitable marriage."

I did laugh, a dry, hooting, out-of-control sound. "Why did he think I wanted his money?" I said.

"Everyone wants money," Dillon said.

I was ready to run out and marry some unsuitable person immediately, just to get him rolling over in his newly dug grave.

"The thing about Fascists," I said, "they're all about control."

"Let's keep politics out of this," Cecie said.

"He was worried about gold-diggers, I think," Dillon said.

Had he left me that much gold?

"I'd like to sign whatever it is," I said, "that gives up my rights to anything. You guys can have it. I don't want to have to deal with this again."

Dillon said, "It's more than you think, Billy boy. And you're young. Late thirties isn't old. You might want to buy a house, send a kid to college."

Want what? I had just been grousing about the measly extra bucks for my airfare. And my life was spent trying to get boosts in pay for undervalued workers. Money wasn't nothing. I knew that as well as anyone. Better than some.

But I was entirely sure about not taking any of however much there was from my father; there was no argument in my head. I didn't want my hand in that till.

Hadn't I decided all this years ago? I only wished I could say this to my father. "Not interested, sorry. Not at all." It was then that I really got that he was gone. I could hardly breathe from the weight of it. He wasn't coming back, no matter what I said. Discussion over.

"Think about it," Cecie said.

"He knew I didn't want it," I said. I had no idea what my father actually thought. But I hated that my sister and my brother assumed I had to take it.

"You were always so stubborn," Cecie said.

I was? Maybe my father meant it kindly, this last begrudging inclusion of me. A man I hadn't seen in seventeen years. But I had been right to get away; I had always been right about that.

"The lawyer can draw up something for me to sign," I said.

When I got back to New York that night, I called all my friends to tell them I was home and why. "So sorry," they said. "Very sorry to hear." But I didn't tell a single person about the will; I didn't think anyone would get it. It was too complicated to explain and too particular to my odd little family. People never get it about money.

Of course, I felt rich for turning it down. You could list all the things you didn't need and feel wonderful for abandoning them. I lay around my apartment for days, watching crappy TV at all hours, renting videos, eating takeout, reading mysteries, having my own little mourning party.

"You look like hell, you must've had a great time," my boss said when I came back to work. I had been drinking too much in the last nights of what was left of my vacation. I wasn't that tan either.

"So does everybody over there hate Americans?" somebody asked.

"Not especially," I said. "Not anymore. End of an empire."

I had to think that this was the great anxiety my father

had lived with, the decline of America as a big fat world power, head of the gluttonous Western world. He lived in anguish at the constant evidence it was slipping, slipping.

Empires slipped. Who didn't know that?

When I traveled in Asia, sometimes people thought I was from Australia or Canada. Too scruffy and penny-pinching to be a rich American. Could I have been rich if I'd held my hand out for the will? Probably not, if interest was all I got. How much was it? I was never going to ask. I was not going to think about it.

And I didn't. Somewhat to my own surprise, I came close to putting it out of my mind, once I signed the form. I didn't hang out with people who did a lot of spending, and I'd never expected to come into money.

What did I need? Not that much. I had my Boston pals—we still talked on the phone—and I had my buddies at work. I thought I got along with everyone, but maybe I didn't. At work there were battles about whether to merge with the Service Employees International Union—I thought this was an okay idea, but I kidded around too much during these battles, I was too jokey and sarcastic. Organizational issues seemed silly to me, though we were based on the deeper need to organize. I made a wisecrack to the wrong person about super-unions and size mattering, and I got switched to a different unit where my workdays were miserable.

Nobody fired me, but I saw I'd have to leave. I hadn't really held that many jobs in my life, and I was not glad about this. Did I want to move into a nonprofit that paid even less? The thing about working, if you think too much about it, is you never want to do any of it. I was at a low point, grouchy and sloppy, when I quit before I meant to, fell into the useless habit of sleeping all day, got evicted from my apartment, camped out with an irritable ex-girlfriend, and spent ten months being a sodden pain in the ass to all. Living off the girlfriend too.

What got me out of it? In the winter I thought I saw my sister on the street, on Fifth Avenue of all places. A woman with her short Republican haircut had two boys with her, one a young teenager and one around ten, and they were looking into the Christmas windows of Saks. Had Cecie put on more weight? It wasn't Cecie, I saw that in a minute, though not before the woman got an alarmed look on her face as if I were stalking them. An unshaven guy in a wool cap, with longish hair sticking out of it, how bad could I look? That bad? And suppose she knew Cecie in New Jersey and was going to go back and tell her? I knew this was an absurd idea, but I was stuck in it.

I went home and cleaned up, I combed and shaved. I got my one suit pressed—"you look like a losing politician," my girlfriend said—and I went out for interviews again. I explained that in the months I hadn't worked I'd been taking care of my sick brother. He was better now, thanks for asking. I said that the union had taught me that the balance between wages, productivity, and profit in our system was totally out of whack. Also that power was never given; it had to be taken. I sounded pretty good.

In time I got a job for an outfit that helped the formerly incarcerated. A job I got to like. My father would really have hated this one, though I hadn't picked it to harass his former self. I was good at it too.

My mother, who was in excellent health, wrote to me, "I wish you weren't always in the profession of telling people the world owes them a living." What old phrases she had. What old wishes. The world, with all its wild shifts and flaring upheavals, was not a changeable planet to her.

For a while, after I moved out from the ex-girlfriend, I stayed away from women. I didn't even do it on purpose, but I had a different sense of my fate. I was better off in my own company, a form I understood. I was better off not entering into false agreements. I wouldn't have won any prizes for celibacy during this time, but I was mostly on my own. How welcome my own place was, when I turned the lock and walked into it at night.

I was trying to get a gig for a newly released individual when I met Rachel. The guy had a chance to get hired as a dishwasher in a hotel kitchen. Rachel did not do the hiring, but she oversaw the contracts. She was at her desk eating a jelly donut the morning I met her and she had a very poised way of chomping as she listened to me. We had a frank discussion of risk and violence and best guesses, and she waved Anthony in.

"You don't get to choose what you're born into," she said. "I have a kid who lives with me who had highly imperfect parents."

"I didn't get along so well with mine," I said, "though I guess they tried. Some don't even try."

The kid who lived with her was eleven and the girl was obsessed with video games. I said I knew about video games and maybe Rachel and I could discuss this over a drink sometime.

She thought we might, and I didn't realize until we were sipping margaritas three days later that she'd sort of thought I might be an ex-con, doing the work that I did. Good for her, I thought, to have a bit of booze with me nonetheless.

I knew zilch about video games, but she never called my bluff. She liked me.

"She wants to spend money," Rachel said, about the kid who lived with her. "Just to have something expensive. Video crap or clothes by designers she thinks every person on earth has heard of."

"What do you do about it?"

Rachel shrugged. "It's her allowance. She can buy stupid things if she saves up."

How supple that shrug was. Sanity is much sexier than people tend to think.

Once Rachel and I got going, I got along with the kid too. Nadia was a sly young thing who laughed at my jokes, and I could imitate both Kelly Clarkson and Beyoncé. People always thought I must not like kids since I'd never bothered to have any. I might be uncharmed by the word *family* but I liked kids fine. Nadia was a hoot.

Rachel had inherited her from an ex-boyfriend, though it was wrong to say "inherit" since Nick, the ex, was still very much alive. Rachel's correction of this term took pride in her act of free will, in her choosing Nadia. "Does *inherit* mean 'automatic'?" I said.

"Nadia doesn't want people thinking her father is dead," Rachel said. "She's still attached to him, you know."

◆ ◆ ◆

One thing I loved to do with Rachel was take her to neighborhoods where I could show her stuff from the parts of the world I loved. In Queens, we went to the Filipino neighborhood in Woodside and the Malaysian food stores in Flushing and the Thai places in Elmhurst. She'd been to Thailand, in her youth. Liked the Golden Treasure restaurant, my favorite, with its great food and great hostess. The Thai had this amazing Buddhist temple—a plain New York brick building with a fabulous gold and blue Thai pagoda roof set on the top and more gold arched over the doorway. We saw monks slipping in and out, with winter wear under their saffron robes in January. "A mirage," Rachel said.

Were the monks happy? Probably a question outside their categories. Their customs didn't allow for showing much expression, but they looked as if they were going about their business just fine. In Thailand I'd seen young novices in the street smoking cigarettes, but not here. Here the monks seemed privately intent, walking around Queens on their two meals a day, their ancient schedules.

"I hope they're warm enough," Rachel said.

People did without a lot of things, that was for sure. My band of the once incarcerated had all gone for years without privacy or safety or a number of civil rights. They'd contrived their own substitutions, same way they made pruno booze out of fruit and sugar in a garbage bag.

I got along with them, my clients, but sometimes I didn't. They got mad at me for getting them jobs they hated or for not getting them jobs at all. I couldn't do everything. "I'm not a magician," I said one night to Rachel, when I was complaining about my day.

"I hope you don't say that to them," Rachel said. "Defeatism isn't what they need."

What a churchy thing for her to say. What did she know about what I dealt with? We fell into a fight, with serious words back and forth about the defects of each other's characters. I really did not want to hear from her what I heard.

We didn't split up from one battle but we cooled on each other. It was better not to talk so often, so we went longer without calling. We expected less from each other, came down from our earlier enthusiasms. We weren't always at our best in public either. Nadia said, "I liked you better before." I snapped at Nadia too. And when it did seem that we were done for as a couple, once and for all, we had a sudden intense revival of interest, a hot reunion. This happened more than once.

We were back and forth for a couple of years, in that way. "It's embarrassing," Rachel said, when we were on good terms, meaning we were really too old for this sort of thing. The truth was, we liked each other, usually. People always said that, didn't they: maybe we should've been just friends. As if longing could be put away.

She stood me up when I wanted to take her to a picnic in Prospect Park with my old union cronies. She had to go somewhere with Nadia; she forgot to let me know. And then I wanted to be alone when she needed me to come to some dinner for her brother. I said I'd come and I didn't.

But that wasn't why I left New York. We were over by then. I left New York in 2008, right in the midst of the financial crisis, because I lost my job. Not just me, the whole outfit went under, its funding petered out. The board had been holding it together, begging for government grants, cajoling private donors—they were giving up now. At the meeting where they broke the news, we all made cracks about the relief of not visiting any more clients in those smelly city shelters. We weren't relieved at all.

Above my desk in the office was a photo of me on a motorcycle on a road with thickly forested mountains on both sides, in Laos, outside Luang Prabang. People were always impressed when I uttered place-names in Asian languages, but I knew nothing. Nothing! Random tidbits. What do tourists ever know? I started looking at job listings overseas.

There were expats working all over Southeast Asia, but the place that had the most NGOs was Cambodia. Other countries had reasons to limit what foreigners could do (Laos and Vietnam were technically still Communist), but Cambodia needed all the help it could get. It was still gutted from the last generation's genocidal war, with one in five Cambodians living below the world poverty line.

Form-letter rejections flooded my email—was I too old, was that it? Okay, I was old. Fifty-three isn't boyhood. But after a much longer spell than I expected, I got Skype-interviewed by an outfit in Phnom Penh that worked with local labor unions to advance worker rights. A job I actually was suited for, no wonder they offered me a contract. I promised I would learn Khmer, I promised everything.

My mother thought I was crazy to go. She thought the Khmer Rouge would kill me, despite my telling her they'd been out of power for more than twenty years.

"I'm off to the glorious East," I said. "That's not so bad."

"You always lived in a fantasy world," she said. My mother was well into her eighties now, with contempt for anyone not as alert as she was.

I told her Phnom Penh was the capital of a real country. I had a Delta Air Lines ticket to it.

"You always think you have the secret to paradise," she said.

She imagined I had secret plans; that was really what she meant. As if I were a dreamy teenager, climbing out through the window, to the freer parts of the neighborhood. Mountaineering for world revolution.

Some friends said they envied my going off into the sunset—how free I was, how brave—and some said, "Well, you have nothing to keep you here," which meant they thought they were better off. I reminded them all that I was going for work, not vacation, into a city of one and a half million, not a tropical garden. My pay was going to go far, but I wasn't going to be lounging around in a bed of orchids.

All the same, Phnom Penh was a big jolt. A modern Asian city, with high-rises and traffic lights and historic temples, that looked like a washed-up village, lined with vendors' carts and tattered awnings and soot-streaked walls and not one foot of unbroken sidewalk. Motorcycles and bikes and tables and unpacked crates were all over the sidewalk anyway—that was how they used it. The city was kind of great in its way, but not what I expected.

In the first weeks I had to get used to what they wanted at work. We were in a campaign that involved sending missives to government agencies about how fucking hot the garment factories were. They answered, we answered back. We bothered American companies (including one that made coats my mother used to wear), but they all pretended they knew nothing of what went on over there. The old hands in the office—kids in their twenties, Americans and Euros—took me out drinking at night; they wanted me to like Phnom Penh. A glass of beer was a dollar, and they knew places where it was even less. I liked the bars—I always liked bars—and I could never decide between the cool ones by the river and the cheaper ones by the market. Everybody thought I was settling in very nicely.

Did I mind being the oldest person in the room? At times I did. The Cambodians in the office (we had a few) included two sisters close to my age, but they never went to bars. I felt I was becoming a marooned colonial senior, far from home, staring into his lager, ready to talk to any idiot.

In some neighborhoods, when I walked out of a bar after midnight, I was stopped by kids who were begging—a little girl carrying her infant brother or a very scrawny boy in a shredded T-shirt. Night was work time for them. The official word was to avoid giving money to children because it encouraged adults to send them out. I didn't always follow the rule. Kids got hit if they didn't bring home enough; you could see that in a second.

My pals at work talked about this—who gave, who didn't. The Cambodians wanted me to know that many, many kids in poverty had very devoted parents, who worked long hours at anything they could. The factory women we advocated for, many of them were mothers. "Don't get wrong idea," the Cambodian sisters said.

If a *barang* like me—a foreigner—wanted a woman, there were plenty of suggestions about where to find one. I stopped fellow drinkers who quoted prices. Not that. I began to think of old girlfriends, ones I'd really liked. Lizzie, for instance. Being around all these twentysomethings full of intelligent, half-baked opinions made me think of her and the kind of talk that went on in that apartment— our flashy, overtalked theories, our delight in whatever we said.

I went online to see if I could find Lizzie. I googled her, and there were several women with her name—one in New Jersey that I got excited about—but they were all the wrong ages. I checked Facebook and LinkedIn, no luck. I had an email message all written in my head, ready to send when I found her. *Saying hi after all these years, hope you're well. I'm working now in Cambodia, very hot weather but you would like it here.*

I sent friends at home my photos of Angkor Wat, once I had enough time off to go there. What dazzled me beyond the temples and the carvings were the maps I kept seeing of the Khmer Empire, which had once ruled most of Southeast Asia. Six hundred years of power, until Angkor (including the largest city in the preindustrial world) was razed by a Thai kingdom in 1431.

Of course, I felt strongly that the whole idea of empire was fucked-up. You had only to look at soldiers leading captives with ropes around their necks in the beautiful temple carvings. When I expounded on this in a bar in Phnom Penh—"not so glorious really"—a young Brit next to me said, "I guess you didn't grow up on *Star Wars*. And the Vikings! Everybody always wants to conquer everybody else."

I wondered what the Khmer Rouge had grown up on. There were probably people I could've asked.

"I'm a leftist," I said. "I'm against rapacious conquest."

The guy looked at me as if I had just said something in Finnish. "What?" he said.

Rachel would have laughed herself silly at someone invoking *Star Wars* in a moral argument. I missed her quite a lot just then.

✦ ✦ ✦

I moved my lodgings pretty often—three apartments in four years. Condo construction took over the cheaper neighborhoods near work, until I landed in Toul Tom Poung, a district with great shopping, by the Russian Market—named in the eighties when its goods and customers came from the Soviet Union. Another empire gone.

In my cozy apartment I watched CNN on TV with a very pretty woman named Clarice who was much too young for me and had talked herself into being smitten with me as the dean of local lore (my Khmer had gotten better). It was the winter of 2016, when Republicans were fighting to be nominated—Ben Carson, Ted Cruz, Carly Fiorina—who even were these people? A reporter interviewed a Tea Party spokesman, who went on about American "exceptionalism" and our natural dominance as "the shining city on the hill" (phrases I knew). Bald, with a cleft chin. Did I know this guy? Why did I think so? I waited for the name. It was Will! My friend from elementary school!

"I used to race toy cars with that guy!" I told Clarice. "He was my best friend till I was twelve."

"I guess he's changed a bit."

"No," I said. And I had to explain how we were raised, the two of us.

"I can't imagine having parents like that," she said.

"They must've been pretty crazy. People like that shouldn't be around children. I think, personally."

"They weren't crazy," I said. "They took care of us. You have it totally wrong."

"Excuse me?" she said. "I can have an opinion."

"You're talking about my parents," I said.

I hated her, I noticed. A growing outrage was coursing hotly under my skin. I could not believe the sheer effrontery of her. Life is full of surprises.

It was around this time that I starting writing to Rachel. A voice out of the blue and it's not even your birthday. How are you these days, how is the ever-amazing Nadia? I'm looking at the sunset on the river. You would really like it here.

For all I knew she was married to someone else by now. We hadn't been a couple for a good nine years. Her answer didn't sound married. She was cheerful and made cracks about how much worse the subway was these days. Nadia had been through a pain-in-the-ass phase but was coming out of it fine. *So good to hear from you*, she said.

I felt better at once for having her with me, despite the inconvenience of her being eighty-eight hundred miles away. She was in my mind when I went about the frustrating tasks of my much-loved job. Which I wished I were a genius at. I wrote, *It's still like nineteenth-century Britain in those factories. Women faint from lack of ventilation. We've had strikes, two years ago five workers got shot. Wages better though than when I started.*

I thought of her when I took my walks. I knew what Rachel would think about the tuk tuk guy who drove like an Italian or the exercise class with blaring music in the park next to Wat Botum. I kept telling her she should come visit. Dick, my friend at work, told me I was making the place sound like Paris and she might notice it was more like Detroit. "A lot of people love Detroit," I said.

In fact I'd grown very loyal to Phnom Penh, where I now had certain trusted buddies, experienced fellow nomads, including a French couple who gave great dinners and a Brit with ironic theories. Dick called it our cadre.

Was I the only one utterly surprised when the old clown with his orange hair was actually nominated? *At least we'll finally have a woman president*, Rachel wrote. *We're so behind the rest of the world.*

On the morning of November 9, when the election headlines blazed across my computer, I could only think that I'd been away so long, I didn't understand a single molecule of anything anymore. Rachel wrote, *I wish I could wake up from this. On the subway a woman was weeping while she looked at her phone. We're in a different part of history now.*

I had to remind her of other elections full of bad news

and worse to come. *Ronald Reagan. Warren Harding. Millard Fillmore* (name always got a laugh). I did find it comforting to think of bad ideas the country had survived.

As it happened, I was living in a place that had lost close to a quarter of its population to a bad idea, worse than bad. Cambodians didn't talk about it right away, but when you knew them they did. Older ones did.

So we're drinking more, Rachel wrote.

I sent her a photo of a can of Angkor Beer. The Cambodian sisters in the office, though they never went to bars, had a brother who sold us crates of the stuff for our little celebrations. The label had a drawing of the temple's three towers on it.

Everyone knows, I wrote to Rachel, *this too will pass.*

That winter I kept sending Rachel photos of palm trees and orchids and any big tropical flower I saw. Who wants icy weather? I thought they would look tempting to her, beckon her to escape.

My brother just got a bad diagnosis, she wrote in one message. It was cancer, and not any kind you'd want. I remembered her brother, a quietly funny guy, and I said how sorry I was. Pretty soon she wasn't writing nearly as often. I became one of those jerks always checking his email. I started to think that we could be Skyping, why weren't we

Skyping? (Because I hated it, but that was an outdated reason.) I didn't want her to slip away.

How exactly like herself she looked on the screen, except that people can never be remembered exactly. It felt stagey, at first, trying to talk, and then we got the hang of it. "Nadia wants to be a designer," she said. "How cool is that," I said. She was talking to me from twelve hours earlier, she was night and I was day. We waved at the end, as if we were going off on different trains.

And that was the beginning of a great habit. We had crucial chats across the time zones, not in the flesh but not invisible either. I watched her explain the particulars of the chemotherapy her brother was getting. She told me the latest Trump jokes. I talked about going for a weekend to Kampot, a couple of hours away and green and quiet. I sent her a photo of a hammock on a beach. We got used to having these conversations. Someday she would visit, we both said. (Not soon, not with her brother this way.)

Some foreigners went home every year or so, but I wasn't one of them. I did send word by email. My mother was getting frailer and looked sadly scrawny in her pictures. *She still knows what's what,* my brother wrote. I sent him a shot of me in front of the royal palace—filigreed gold roof with curling finials, white columns, me in shorts—and when he showed it to her, she said, "It doesn't look so poor there. Do they need him?"

My father hated poor people. He thought they brought on their own misery by irresponsible habits and misguided decisions and then they complained all the time and wanted special favors. He truly believed that wealth was a sign of good judgment and right behavior, and that free market forces naturally brought about justice.

It was a utopian notion really—without interference, true freedom would exist as it was meant to. He loved freedom. The demonic forces of interference were always lurking.

At work one of the new hires, a twenty-six-year-old from Miami, had her purse snatched by a guy on a motorcycle riding by. She was knocked off her feet by the speed and roughness of the grab and was badly shaken—she had screamed from the sidewalk. She came to work with bandages on her arm and leg, where she'd hit the pavement going down. Clarice, my ex-friend, said, "I had that happen once too. It can be very fucked-up here."

"It's getting worse," someone said. Someone always said that, all the years I'd been here. What did they know? Okay, there were more foreigners now, with more money to take.

I remembered my own brief life as a thief—episodes of minor shoplifting, culminating in the entirely insane adventure of scaling the fake-castle restaurant in Vermont. I could've killed myself! I'd been in real terror up there, and then the thrill of finding the cash box inside. The bills that would fuel my escape.

I was moved to tell this story to Rachel the next time we were having a conversation on Skype. Telling made me come up with lots of details. Three stories up and some of the shingles were loose under my grip. I'd had to concentrate so, so hard, as I crawled and clung. "What a hoodlum," she said. "I'm sorry I didn't know you then."

Definitely one of the better things anyone ever said to me. I was holding on to it, trying to keep the way she said it, while I took one of my walks at the end of the day. I was going along the riverbank, around to the spot where the Tonlé Sap met the Mekong, as I waited for the air to turn cooler. The water was calm and silvery, and as the sky went from pinkish mist to gray dusk, the lights came on along the tourist boats.

My father had once talked about buying a boat, though he'd never done any such thing and wasn't on the water very much. In fact he rarely took vacations. Sometimes now it struck me that I'd been hard on my father—he had been hard on me too, very (I still thought that)—but I had been stubborn and enraged and unforgiving. I admired myself for it, too. I did still. When I pictured my father in my head, I had no interest in offering apologies, but I had great sadness at the thought of him. What a battle we had made about everything.

I was sorry it couldn't have been otherwise; I might have said that much at least. (It was not easy to imagine this conversation.) And I would have wanted him to know, of course, that things had turned out well for me; it might not look that way but they had. Here I was, taking in the luxury of an evening walk along the byways of an Asian city, gazing at the lights of settlement on an ancient waterway, pleased at the form of my days. I had honorable work in a part of the world I loved; a beautiful woman was blessing me over the internet. *I couldn't ask for more than I have*, I would have told him.

6 / Tara

My mother almost got married when she was nineteen. As she told it, she was a townie that Gil (she liked saying his name) was fooling around with in New Brunswick. He went to Rutgers, and they'd met because she was working as a receptionist for a local New Jersey doctor he went to for a torn rotator cuff. She flirted with a lot of the patients; nobody cared in those days. It was midway into the sixties.

What he liked about her was her lack of timidity (a trait she kept). Their best date was a trip to Asbury Park—he'd never met a girl who wanted to go on the roller coaster two times in a row. All the crazy lurching, the swoops and the turns and the insane dips they could see ahead but couldn't stop from happening were to her an orchestrated metaphor for the great physical excitement they were privately carrying on whenever they could. She'd been to the park many times as a kid, but on these visits she really understood it. It was a gaudy version of an enormous truth. She explained this to me with more specifics than I wanted.

So she and Gil were out on a warm May evening, right before the end of the semester, and they were strolling the boardwalk with their french fries and red cream sodas after the rides. "You know what?" he said. "You could marry me."

My mother was wildly flattered—no one had proposed to her before—and she didn't even really mind the conceited way he phrased it. But the finality of marriage (marriage!) didn't seem accurate to her for what they had, though she was willing to be open-minded. "Maybe we should live together first?" she said. Since dropping out of college she'd been living at home and was eager not to.

"Forget it then," he said.

She hadn't known how insulted he would be. He stopped right there on the boardwalk and turned around and walked them back to the parking lot, a long and winding walk (it took her a minute to stop thinking: *No frozen custard?*). "We don't have to *leave*," she said. "Are we leaving? Don't leave!"

He hated anything she said then, no matter how tearful she got. "I should've known," he kept saying. "You're such an infant, you have no clue at all." She hadn't expected him to turn on her like that. They had more dates before they actually broke up, but that was the end of whatever good times they had.

✦ ✦ ✦

Years later, after my mother had lived all over the world, she was shopping in New York for a jacket, and she saw Gil's name on a label. She knew it was really Gil, she knew he'd gone into the clothing business, but still it was a shock to see the threaded letters in satin. "I knew I couldn't buy the jacket," she said. "Nothing against Gil, but nobody wants the past muttering to her every time she gets dressed. Does she?"

The next boyfriend she had, after Gil, saw how well situated she was for swiping a few boxes of pharmaceuticals from the doctor's office. She didn't think anyone would catch her and they didn't. She packed the goods neatly in her tote bag, under a flowered silk scarf. "Good girl," Quinn, the boyfriend, said. She'd expected heartier praise, and he didn't kiss her until after he'd counted the bottles. She was excited anyway. She wanted to be a different sort of person and he was offering lessons.

He'd wanted the drugs to sell, not use, though they did try them and get stoned and drowsy and physical (as they called it then) in slow ways. They were in his apartment at the time, in another part of her town. She fell asleep and didn't go home to her parents' house till morning, and the ruckus when she walked in, all the shouting and insults, caused her to see that she really could not live there anymore.

So Quinn was her ticket out (somewhat to his surprise). They had to move her belongings from the family home during her lunch hour, when no parent was in sight; he came in his car to get her and her duffle full of clothes. She was so young some of them still had nametapes from camp. And then he was picky where she put them in his closet.

She got along with everyone at the doctor's office, she had a good personality, so no one worried if she spent a few minutes in the back closet, getting her hands on a few more drugs Quinn knew the names of. She went slow on the thefts, small amounts each time; she saw the risks. Quinn would have had her trucking out every bit of stock in uppers or downers they had. Let him call her chicken-shit if he wanted; limits were needed. She brought a bunch of daffodils to the office by way of apology the day she explained to the good doctor (he wasn't that good) that she had to leave very soon to go back to school. "Pre-law," she said. "It'll be a grind." Who goes to school in April? No one said a word. Her new zest for falsity did nothing but pay off.

Quinn was furious that she'd quit without even consulting him. "What am I supposed to do now?" he said.

"I have to tell you," she said. "I might have a job in London."

One advantage of working for a doctor who treated

sports injuries was that a lot of men came through the door. She'd been having a thing with someone named Matthew, who had hurt his knee hiking the Kittatinny Ridge. He wanted to start off in England and go on the overland route across Europe to Asia—take buses or trains or hitch rides on trucks—through Turkey and Iran and Afghanistan, as far as the Himalayas. It would take them months but it wouldn't cost much. My mother wanted something but she didn't know what, and this was the best theory she'd heard, the most ambitious. She had a little money from her share of the drug profits, to get them started, and he was selling a car he had.

"What kind of job?" Quinn said.

"In a hotel," she said. "My cousin knows someone in this London hotel."

She must have been slightly afraid of Quinn to announce her leaving in this way. And leave she did. He called her names but he didn't stop her, and she went back to her parents just for a few days (her family was still mad she hadn't stayed with Gil) and then she slipped off for good with dear Matthew. A man with a generally nice character, though my mother had no idea then really. He'd found a cheap charter flight to London, and she even liked the crummy airline food, she was so excited. She fell asleep on his shoulder with the tray still in front of her. And that was how I came to spend the first nine years of my life in Nepal.

My mother's name was Frances but everyone called her Frankie. They named me Tara, after a figure of great powers in Tibetan Buddhism—lucky for me it sounded like a regular name, though I had a phase of trying to be called Terry. My sister got stuck with Apsara, which was harder to tell people.

I had a cheerful childhood really. In Kathmandu my parents' friends thought kids were intriguing creatures and they could easily be induced to play with us; they believed in freedom, in the rights of kids to run around like little maniacs. Apsara and I had each other to run with, we had buddies who came and went, and sometimes we got to play with the Nepali kids on our street. We had enough language for simple games and they didn't mind us.

There were a few episodes of neglect. Once we got lost for hours taking a shortcut through the alleys of the city and were really scared, and once my sister had a cut that got infected and left some nerve damage in her foot. But mostly the joy and wonder that the grownups were in the business of hunting down was quite compatible with our preferences. My father taught us to read, when he was home from his hikes, and when he had bits of cash from setting up other travelers with mountain routes and trekking guides, we were sent to a little school run by an Englishwoman. It was almost like a real school.

Of course, they couldn't stay in Nepal forever. California was a big shock when we landed there. We were staying in Berkeley, as good a spot as they could've picked, camping out in the living room of a friend of my father's from college. People were perfectly nice to us, but they had different customs. School was much worse than we expected. My sister and I were not used to being apart and had no experience sitting still at desks for two and a half hours in the morning and two and a half hours in the afternoon. My sister was the one more outraged at first—she screamed and tried to leave by herself—but she adapted sooner. She was only seven; people put up with her.

I was better at doing what they told me, but I stayed horrified. This was really going to keep happening for the next eight years? My father said, "You'll get used to it, chicken. I'm sorry." Eventually I did learn how to give answers in certain subjects (not arithmetic) and then one girl asked me about the food I brought for lunch. I swapped my lentil stew for her cheese sandwich, the way kids do, and after that I could sort of talk to her and some of the others.

I'd seen a few videos on TV screens in Nepal but I'd never seen a movie in a movie theater, the vast glowing spectacle in the monumental dark, sealed and pure. My father's friends took us to see *E.T.* and I couldn't get over it. I came out amazed to be outside again, with all those wild events tucked back into themselves, known from a distance. I loved that distance; I loved being the monarch of my feelings.

My mother had to say, "I still can't get over the way the electricity stays on all the time here." She was having her own identity issues adjusting to the U.S. and tended to mock the ease and convenience of things. My sister kept repeating her favorite lines (*phone home*) from the scenes she liked and I shushed her savagely; I didn't want anyone else's version of what I'd just been through. I should've paid more attention to Apsara.

They were not into money, my parents, but they knew they needed it, now that they'd left their beloved Kathmandu, where prices were set by residents barely used to a cash economy. My father, who always wanted to be outside, was applying to be a park ranger. My mother thought she might start a store where she could sell pashmina shawls. These ideas did not match, but they weren't used to holding jobs and may not have quite noticed. In the meantime, my mother got us food stamps. She said we had to get them fast before Reagan took them away.

It was May when my father finally got his placement in Devils Postpile National Monument. A name that scared us, but he couldn't believe his luck. My mother would've kept all of us in Berkeley, waiting for his visits, but it turned out we did not have lodging forever with his friends. My parents had loud, sharp fights about what real life was, and then my father went off to what she called his hut in the wilderness. And when school was out in June, my mother took Apsara and me on a four-day bus trip (which we mostly liked) to New York. She had a friend from high school who put us up at first, and we settled on the Lower East Side. Someone let her work as a hostess in a restaurant—she liked the sociability and she could bring food home. And that was where we did the rest of our growing up.

Our mother always had to leave for work at four thirty in the afternoon, so our dinners were like after-school snacks. Apsara was the less civilized one, so cute she got away with murder. She ate with her hands, she put Log Cabin syrup on her hamburger; my mother didn't care. When we got older I was in charge of feeding us. We never had sitters (I was already ten) but we had a neighbor we could call. The neighbor kids loved our food.

Nobody we knew had any money. Admittedly, our clothes were more makeshift—the bottom of the Goodwill barrel—but Apsara could spruce hers up with a belt or a zebra-print scarf she cherished. We had protectors when someone decided to mock or threaten us; we had the other kids in our building. In high school I was sometimes scared, but not too often.

I was good at schoolwork. When our father came to visit, maybe twice a year, he always said I was going to be president. He took me to movies; he'd do two in a row if I wanted. (Age suitability was nothing to him; we both liked *Blue Velvet*.) He took Apsara skating, ice in winter and roller in summer. He figured out the forms for my financial aid for college. Even our mother still loved him, though they both had other people, on and off.

The college he helped me pick (in upstate New York, three and a half hours away) was a school full of other movie nuts, a great place, and my theories were no weirder than anyone's. My friend Tracey, a girl from the Bronx who could bat around terms like *master shot* and *eyeline matching*, thought my freshman film about garbage trucks was "much better than most other crap." I was never more thrilled with myself.

A boyfriend I had for a while in my twenties used to say, "I hate to break the news to you, but nobody lives on nothing anymore." I wasn't flaky about money—I was the anti-flaky one in my family—but small amounts always seemed like enough to me. I was a barista at Starbucks when he said this, and I didn't hate the job either. I'd been out of college a few years, trying to get some kind of work on other people's films. Of course, I wanted to make my own, but when would that be? A student film of mine got shown at a festival, I helped with the editing of my friend Tracey's short doc, and I made excellent lattes, with designs in the foam.

At least I was doing better than my sister, who liked to come in for free scones. She was doing too many drugs—I didn't know which drugs, substances with nicknames way beyond me. She didn't look that bad, a skinny pretty girl in a black T-shirt, not unusual. If I took my break at a back table with her, she'd tell me how her boyfriend had disappeared but was probably coming back, and she was getting a job soon really. I could never get her to come stay with me.

I made my first documentary with a grant from the state of New York and with lots of friends helping. It was about the innocent lives of urban rats; I had good close-ups of their squirrel-like activities and recorded talk from experts who didn't hate them. Unsensational and fascinating, that was my pitch. The hard part was getting it shown anywhere. Tracey helped me get it into an evening of films by women, and the audience applauded after it was over. We got a few other showings too.

The rats worked for free, but the next project needed more cash. I wanted to do something about the Triangle Shirtwaist Factory fire that killed 146 garment workers in 1911. Most of the victims had lived on my old streets on the Lower East Side and in what was now the East Village. I had this plan of also filming the cotton fields in the South where the cloth came from, maybe with old stills of the pickers. And I wanted footage of boll weevils. My camera-person had to be good.

Filmmakers—the ones I knew, the doc people—were always talking about the burden of raising money. How super-hard it was now, at the end of the nineties. I knew I had to sound relevant but original to foundations public and private and be eloquent with rich people, convincing them that leftist documentaries were wonderfully in keeping with who they were. If they didn't fund me this year, they'd do it the next.

I didn't give up; I kept trying. I was not rewarded for this.

✦ ✦ ✦

My mother said, "You need a rich boyfriend."

"Mom," I said, "you really think I could nab a sugar daddy? And I don't see you dating any fat cats yourself."

"I had my boyfriend, Gil," she said, "when I was young. Now he's a big deal. You know how many coats he sells?"

"I don't," I said, "and you don't either."

"He wanted to marry me. You could find him. There's the internet."

"Mom."

"I don't mean as a lover. I mean as an investor. It's so easy nowadays, with email. People's companies have websites. You go through a few offices, you can get through. I've already had a little back-and-forth with him, and I don't have your computer skills. He was very glad to hear from me."

"You found him? The guy Gil?"

"Just a little hi-how-are-you. He travels a lot in Malaysia. All the factories are overseas now, you know. I was never in Malaysia. People say it's great."

"Maybe he'll let me film his factories."

"Wouldn't that be funny?" my mother said.

✦ ✦ ✦

My mother thought Gil would be interested because he was Jewish and the Triangle fire had a great number of Jewish victims. (Also plenty of Italians.) "Does he give money for these things as a habit?" I said.

She was sure he did, but when I looked this up as well as I could, it seemed to be one of her illusions.

"He's dying to meet you. And Apsara too," my mother said.

I understand my mother (Frankie) has been in touch with you, I said in my email. I explained my history as an innovative filmmaker—I sent a link to a trailer he could look at—and I suggested (was this creepy?) that a contemporary manufacturer of clothing would have insights that might be of help to me on this project. Also, I looked a lot like my mom, if he wanted to see on my website.

He wrote back, *I am glad to know she has creative children. I have a son and a daughter just a little younger than you. My boy is in law school. Doing well.*

I said he was lucky to have work that took him overseas. He wrote, *I enjoy Asia. Malaysia and Indonesia are very nice. Thailand was even nicer. But I miss my wife and family.*

I wrote, *I am interested in textile manufacture as a result of my research (which, by the way, could always use funding). Can you tell me anything that might be of use about current practices in garment factories where you are?* It was a rash question, but I didn't say anything about forced overtime or poor ventilation or underage workers.

As you are surely aware, he wrote a few days later, *we do require basic standards, better than basic, but once you're dealing with the Third World much is out of your hands. I'm sure you understand that having grown up in Nepal.*

"What do you want from me?" was what he was saying. The answer was "money" but I wasn't going to say that. I already knew better. A person doesn't have to humiliate herself every single second. I could spare us both.

I loved Nepal, I wrote. *Apsara did too. People think we've forgotten but we haven't.*

I was thinking of the two of us running around those streets—they were so bare of cars. Even the bicycle rickshaws were always waiting for fares, hoping. But the marketplace was crowded—people bargaining and pushing their way through to the stalls. Apsara almost got stepped on, more than once. How eternal markets were, the buzz of commerce. *Best price for you, special today:* heard throughout history. Was I unfair to Gil?

How prosperous Gil was, compared to Nepal—how hard it was for him to enter the kingdom of heaven, easier for a camel to pass through the eye of a needle. Out of his hands, my ass.

I thanked him for corresponding with me. I would let

him know the next time a film of mine was showing in New York.

My mother thought Apsara could be a great pre-K teacher, if she ever went back to school to get a degree. She liked little kids; she'd be a natural. This was my mom's idea, not Apsara's. In the meantime she was living with another deadbeat boyfriend and taking people's coats in a club. She was glad to be working nights, sleeping late. We were all late sleepers.

I had a shooting script for the first part of my Triangle fire movie. Even Apsara had to listen to me talk about it. The original building now belonged to NYU, with a plaque citing its history. At the time of the fire, doors on the ninth floor were kept locked so workers going home could be searched for stolen goods. I made her hear how trapped factory girls (younger than us, mostly) jumped out the windows from nine stories up, clothes and hair on fire, some of them holding hands.

She said, "I once had a suicide pact. With Jinx, remember her?"

"Oh, no," I said. "Fuck. What were you going to do?"

"I can't remember."

"Bullshit. You remember."

"Oh, well," she said. "We were just going to put rocks in our socks and go jump off the pier at Coney Island. At night. We didn't mean it."

Jinx was her high school friend. What else had I missed?

"Now, Terry," she said, "you always get so carried away about everything. No big deal. Really."

In Nepal, when she was little, my sister had been such a bubbly, active creature. Her name (she liked it then) meant something like "celestial dancer," so she was always twirling around and skipping and hopping, a soft-shoeing angel. When she cut her foot she made up a hoppity lift-the-left dance step. I had been moodier, harder to please. Who knew where happiness came from? Well, actually, there were theories. In the Buddhism my father sometimes followed you heard arguments on the vanity of grasping for happiness. Whatever you ran after and clung to was destined to slip out of your hands, melt like snow, dissolve into thin air. What could be more obvious? The truth of impermanence was somehow a cheering idea to my father. He scoffed at the penny-ante ambitions most people knocked themselves out for. He believed in freedom, my father.

◆　◆　◆

The next week I tried asking Apsara, "So do you know how Jinx is now?"

"Jinx has a kid, she lives in Philadelphia."

"She's okay?"

"Why wouldn't she be?"

My sister had to get off the phone, she was on her way to the club, big big night, huge crowds, because the so-and-so's were coming, a group I'd never heard of. "I'm ignorant," I said.

"The last time they came Wilton danced for three and a half hours straight." Wilton was her boyfriend.

"I'm so out of it."

"You'd love them," she said, and she laughed. Maybe she had a better life than I did.

My mother almost died having me. The hospital in Kathmandu had hygiene problems and she got a terrible infection. My father was very worried when she was pregnant the second time and he borrowed the money to fly us to Bangkok ten weeks in advance. I didn't remember any of it, of course, since I was only two, but apparently I was a total pain in Thailand. "I didn't want to leave Nepal either," my mother said. "Big fuss for nothing." She was really quite brave, my mother.

In Thailand I almost drowned in the Chao Phraya

River. I was playing on the shore and slipped; it took them a minute to notice me spluttering. "Imagine that," I told my friend Tracey. "I had a near-death experience before I was even talking in full sentences."

"It doesn't really count if you don't remember," she said.

But I thought it did. I had it as a story, passed down. I knew it so well, had always known it.

It turned out boll weevils were not a factor in the Triangle Factory's cotton supply. The big invasion of ravenous bugs from Mexico didn't get into full swing until the twenties, at least a decade later. I really wanted to keep the weevils in the action. Audition the best chewers, show off their talents.

Not my best idea. Where else could I go with this? The owners of the Triangle Shirtwaist Company had actually been brought to trial for manslaughter. They hired a great lawyer and were acquitted. A few years later they were accused of locking the door in another factory.

The fire had likely been started by one of the cutters— the best paid of the workers, all men—tossing a cigarette butt near a bin of cotton scraps and paper patterns; cutters smoked, which was against the rules but tolerated. Male privilege.

You have to think about who's to blame and you'll see more than you even want to, if you're making a movie.

My mother said, "People hate being stolen from. They get outraged in a totally out-of-proportion way. How much could any girl ever have taken from that factory? I mean, bits of lace? Maybe a blouse rolled up? Very small potatoes." My mother had had a few challenges about the amount of food she took home from one restaurant. Apsara was very fond of a cheesecake they were not, apparently, throwing out that night. My mother lost that job. She found another, but it took some doing.

My mom was phoning me now to talk about Apsara. When had I last spoken to her? What did I think about her saying she thought summer was the most depressing season? Summer? What kind of thing was that to say?

"She's fine," I said. "She told me she and what's-his-name, Wilton, go to the beach all the time. Jones Beach, which is not bad, you know."

My mother was going off to Maine for two weeks with a new boyfriend. She was young, our mom, just past fifty, with a full head of very curly dark hair (I had the hair), and she kept herself looking good, a requirement (she thought) of her job. That was where she had met her new guy, who was a prep cook in the kitchen. Quite a bit younger than she was too. "Just watch out for Apsara while I'm gone," she said. As if anyone could really watch her.

"Property is theft," I said to Tracey. We had written this in Sharpie on a wall when we were in college, quoting a nineteenth-century French anarchist (Proudhon, whose name I never heard after). No one could scrub it off. A great sentence, with much behind it.

Tracey said, "What did your mother swipe besides the cheesecake?" I always hated anyone speaking against my mother. Did she think pilfering was something out of *Goodfellas?* Tracey was a friend but we were old rivals too.

"I don't know. All our glasses and cutlery. A nice steel pitcher."

Tracey had a whole set of frying pans from her family's hoard. My parents hadn't carried back any household goods on the plane from Kathmandu; whatever we had here was scavenged and scrounged by my mother.

"Do you ever think of going back to Nepal?" Tracey said. "I mean if you had the money. I'd go with you if you ever went."

Our beloved Nepal was having a nasty civil war—Maoists against other factions, including the royal family.

Did we still know anyone there? I remembered my mother writing to friends. People still wrote letters then.

My sister, who didn't remember the place as well as I did, had the best keepsake. She had a little temple bell made of brass, which I'd always coveted. The Hindu temples around us always had bells ringing and clattering at certain hours. I didn't want to go to Nepal with anyone from here. I didn't think they'd get it.

Tracey had three different sources funding a film she was about to start shooting, about a murder committed by two women who then went trout-fishing in the Catskills. She'd be gone for six weeks, hanging around cool creeks while we sweated in the city. I was way behind her as a filmmaker— well, everyone can't be at the same level, right? I had talent but so did any number of humans. I might never get to do what I wanted. That was a simple fact. I might be one of those people whose projects were always half-thought-through, whose ideas never got off the ground. No one wanted them; the plans vanished. "You can think of something else to do," my mother said. It was one of the worst things she ever said to me.

◆ ◆ ◆

Apsara came in to see me at Starbucks one hot July afternoon. She told me, while I was using the noisy milk steamer, that she wanted to borrow money. "Just three hundred, just for a little while," she said. "I had some extra expenses, I got caught short."

Extra expenses—that's how you talk to your sister who knows you? Apsara was gritting her teeth too, a sign of bad habits. "Yeah, sure," I said. "Come after work, we'll go to the bank."

"Don't you have a break before, just a short one? Couldn't we go right away? Like now?" How childish she sounded, how pesty. I told her to come back in an hour.

"You could just give me the bank card," she said.

"An hour," I said. "Come back then."

She didn't come back. Where the fuck was she? No place good. When I phoned, I just got her voicemail, with a tune behind it. I tried more than once. I called the club but the woman who answered the phone said, "Not here Tuesdays. Sorry," and hung up. I didn't know the boyfriend's last name or the address where she lived with him, if that was where she lived. I hadn't wanted to know. What was the matter with me? I thought of calling hospitals—how many were there in the city? Could I really find anything out? I wasn't calling my mother. Not yet.

Apsara called me around noon the next day to say, "I'm fine. Forget about the loan. Everything's fine. You okay?"

✦ ✦ ✦

My mother had a story about why they left Kathmandu. They had weathered a number of things by then. They'd loved their first months in that beautiful, flamboyant, dirty city, with legal hashish sold in shops all over. They liked hanging out and they liked the simplicity of being high, as if they were an airier and more advanced species. But my father wanted to go on his treks and my mother was so young she thought she could be a fashion designer. She bought beautiful fabrics very cheaply; she cut a pattern out of brown paper and tried sewing by hand, which took forever. My father found her one day, wrapped in a cocoon of brocade, weeping in sodden defeat. "I can't do it," she said, which was true. In the end he rented the top floor of a building with a long balcony, and my mother occupied herself furnishing it with small purchases from the market and having friends over for chai. She loved this part, which went on for a while. Then she got pregnant with me and gave up drugs and bidi cigarettes. She ate a lot of sweets instead, *burfi* and all the sugary, dense, ghee-laden things we later loved.

My mother came so close to dying after I was born that neither she nor my father ever got over it. She said she remembered lying in the dark in the hospital and seeing a shape in the hallway she was sure was a crocodile, waiting to open its jaws, and she couldn't cry out. My father said he was thinking of all he'd done wrong to get them to this spot and he wanted to crawl to each of the nurses to beg forgiveness, though the nurses were part of the cause.

"What a pit that hospital was," my mother said. It didn't, however, embitter them against Nepal. When I was three years old, the Nepali government decided to outlaw cannabis and to drive hordes of hippies down to the border in vans, deporting them to India. My parents weren't living in one of the hotels and nobody ordered them anywhere, and they stayed, happily.

But why did they leave when they did? It was my fault but I didn't know it. I yelled at a little Nepali boy in our yard who dropped a book of mine into the mud. English kids' books were hard to get, and I said vicious, sneering words to him in Newari, a local language I later lost the sounds of. Whatever I said made my mother think we were doing a bad job of living there and I was becoming hideous. They probably wanted to leave anyway; they were probably ready.

I got a phone call from Apsara while I was at my local Laundromat, waiting with a basket of wet clothes for a free dryer. "Hey," she said, "sorry to bother you but I kind of need to borrow money again."

"Why am I the one?" I said.

"You never lent the last time," she said.

"I'm the rich sibling?"

"I just need five hundred. It's not that much. I'll get it back to you soon. You won't even miss it."

Said like a true druggie. I didn't even know what she liked—Ecstasy, Special K, new forms of meth, late-nineties favorites—you'd think I could tell, she was Apsara, but I couldn't. She always swore all she did was drink white wine. Anyone can swear anything.

"How much cash do you think I have floating around?" I said. "I work for Starbucks, not Apple."

"If your friend Tracey needed it for one of her movies, you'd find a way to get it for her," my sister said. Where had that come from? "You're just as cold and fucked-up as every other film person I've ever met. In Nepal you weren't like that."

"You don't even remember. We were little. What *is* this?"

"Stop yelling at me," she said.

"Someone has to yell at you," I said, "because you're going downhill fast. A complete and total train wreck."

I thought the conversation was over, but then I heard myself offer her two hundred, that was the best I could do.

She was cloyingly grateful when she came to my apartment an hour later to pick it up. "Thank you so much, you don't know how much this is appreciated," she said. "Really, really."

"Oh, please," I said. "Don't be creepy."

She was giving me a fake smile. Me, her sister.

227

✦ ✦ ✦

A week later, when my mother came back from her excellent Maine vacation—good chowder, great boyfriend,
ice-cold ocean—she couldn't find Apsara. My sister's cell
phone said that it was not receiving incoming calls. The
club said that no one with that name was working there
at present. My mother knew Wilton's whole name, but no
address was listed anywhere for him. Apsara's old friend
Jenny said she hadn't talked to her for months.

"You were supposed to take care of her," my mother
said to me.

"Oh," I said. "That's my job? She's too old for that
anyway."

"I have to find her. We have no idea where she is. What
if she's lying in the street somewhere?"

"She's fine." I meant it when I said it—I was mad at her
for talking me into a loan—but I knew too well the reasons
she might not be so fine. Bit by bit they leaked out. My
mother moaned.

"I am so disappointed in you," she said.

"Me?" I said. "The world's most casual mother is taking
it out on me. Did you ever pay attention to either of us?"

My mother should not have been as shocked by this as
she was. Her face flinched as if I had whacked her; her eyes
were small and wounded.

"This is the worst side of you," she said.

"You should never have had us," I said. "Why did you bother?"

I asked if she had taken the trouble to call my father, who should've raised us instead of her; maybe he'd heard from Apsara. She dialed him then and there—it was early morning in California—and she handed me the phone while it was ringing. "Hey," my father said, glad to hear my voice. I sputtered out our panic about Apsara, our defeats and frustrations and growing dread. "She went to Baltimore," he said. "She didn't tell you?"

Wilton the boyfriend had family in Baltimore. They were going to stay there for a while till the dust cleared— my father didn't know what the dust was either. There was a landline phone at the boyfriend's family's house; she had given him the number. Just so he wouldn't worry if he tried to reach her.

My mother called the number and left a message and called again enough times so that she got hold of Apsara by the next day. "The thing is," my mother told me later, "I don't like the way she sounds. She sounds foggy and stupid and out of it. What does that mean?"

"What do I know?"

I thought Wilton had probably done well to take her

home. My mother called so often she finally got a different version of events. The story was that Apsara had gotten overheated and dehydrated and what-all from her usual dancing around in a club she liked in Brooklyn. She'd fainted but then they brought her around with ice cubes down her bra and got her home. She thought she was fine at home and she took a few OTC sleeping pills to help her rest. Maybe more than a few. It wasn't till early morning that the boyfriend had big problems waking her and had the sense to bring her to an emergency room.

"They let her go after a *day*," my mother said. "Do you think that's right? I don't think that's right."

Wilton claimed that Baltimore was now doing Apsara a world of good. His family was feeding her banana pudding, which she loved. My mother said Wilton was different than she'd thought. They'd had a good conversation. But nobody wanted us to visit, especially not Apsara herself.

"I left because I wanted to leave," my sister said. "I don't need to bring New York with me."

"We're not her dealers," I said to my mother. "What is she talking about?"

"We need to get her somewhere," my mother said. "You know what I mean. A treatment center."

Did my sister even have insurance? She was no longer employed, for one thing.

"She needs to go someplace good," my mother said. "They have places she'd like. We can find out."

"You know they charge a ton, those places."

"I don't care. What does it matter? We know people," my mother said. "We know Gil. I can write to Gil. You know how many coats he sells?"

Maybe my mother was aware of something I wasn't. Maybe the times she and Gil had together—the times in bed with their new bodily talents, the nights of his telling her what he thought the world should do, the blue evenings of their walking on the boardwalk—were unforgettable and unforgotten. Maybe he would be delighted and honored to help his once-loved Frankie in her later troubles in her interesting life. He had a family; he knew what kids meant. And he was from a generation that liked drugs; he wouldn't think my sister was just a self-destructive idiot. Though I thought that at the moment. My mother would know how to talk to him. She would tell him Apsara had had a hard time because of her restless sprite-like nature and she needed physical activity but she was so sharp at understanding people she would be fine once she focused. Once she got help.

◆ ◆ ◆

My mother actually bragged the next morning about what a good message she'd written to Gil. "I just have a feeling," she said.

Did I believe her? Who knew what to believe? He didn't answer her email right away (why would he?), and then my mother looked up the phone number for his company's office in New York. In case he was there and not in Malaysia.

She got him on the phone the next day. Leave it to Frankie. He'd let the call through. "Your voice sounds like your voice," she told me he said.

"I think about us when I look at my girls," she said. "About being young, I mean."

"It's different for them now."

"I bet you don't look old," she said.

He chuckled. "I wish."

"I have good memories," she said. "You know what I mean."

"I do," he said.

Then she explained again about my sister. She hoped neither of his kids were ever in that kind of danger. It wasn't a thing she could describe. But there were places to help Apsara, she knew there were places. Gil said he was confused about what this had to do with him. "Just a loan," my mother said.

"Oh," he said.

He said he had enough dependents to worry about as

it was. What was it with people remembering him only when they wanted money? He was surprised at Frankie—Frankie of all people, Frankie who had never been like that—but maybe he shouldn't have been, since the other daughter had also wanted a handout.

My mother understood that she had insulted him. He'd been glad that she was calling him, after all these years—the lost girlfriend come back again, trailing new longings, even if he had a wife—and then this nice prospect had turned into a bid for cash. A trick against him. She would have been glad to run over to his office for a quickie if that could've helped Apsara. Too late.

"I remember," she said to him, "when Apsara was born. We went to Bangkok—I don't know if you've ever been there—and the nurses didn't have much English. When they showed her to me, I said, *Kop kun ka*, which was 'thank you,' the only thing I knew in Thai. Everybody laughed. But that was the right thing to say."

"I love Bangkok," he said. "We had factories in Thailand, but not for as long as I would've liked. It's a wonderful country, my favorite. I miss it. I haven't been back for eleven years."

She was thinking what a fortune he must've made—the man was not hurting for money—just as he was reminding her how sorry he was that he was pretty busy at the moment and had to end their conversation.

She was very upset at home that night. She joked about robbing banks, but with my mother you never knew. Could a hacker get into his account, she asked me. A really good hacker, could that person do it?

My sister had some sort of tiff with Wilton and she decided to get out of Baltimore and all that stupid bed rest. She stuffed a backpack with her outfits and talked Wilton's father into driving her to the bus station. Wilton was pissed off when he told us, and he didn't know where she'd gone. Maybe Miami.

"Never thanked any of us," Wilton said.

My mother tried to be calm. "She has to do things her own way, doesn't she? Sometimes that's just how it is." I thought my mother was uttering bullshit.

But maybe not. What did I know? Apsara camped out illegally somewhere in Florida—she sent us one email with a sentence about the surf at night. On the beach she met people—who knew what people—and she got work outside Miami dancing in a club. If she was in a tailspin, we didn't get details; she wrote when she wanted to. We had to get used to her being away. "She's not coming back," I told my mother, just guessing. Apsara did send emails to both of us to check that we were really okay when the World Trade Center came down—we were so glad to hear from her, proud for months. She made friends with someone who was a nanny, and she developed some sort of exercise program for little kids. Kids loved it—they saw her on the beach—and after a while she got paid to run it in municipal parks. My father visited her and had a great time—he said she looked like a punk grasshopper ballerina, in her green leotard, with her hair.

My mother and Ron, the prep cook who took her to Maine, had a longer run than anyone expected. He used to take her to salsa clubs—she loved this—and they went to Maine every summer. I liked him. She never had anybody after that. I met a really good guy in a class I took in digital editing. He helped me write grant proposals (I'd been doing them wrong), and I actually got funding to shoot a doc on the origins of the New York subway and all its barely connected lines. It got more showings and more attention than anyone ever thought, and I had better results getting bits of backing after that. I loved using history, as long as everyone saw the danger of thinking that bad news was over.

For years my mother spoke with remorse about the way she had treated Gil. She had badly wounded him twice—first in showing no eagerness to marry him and second in asking for a loan when he thought she had romance in mind. "I never wanted to hurt his feelings. He never did me any harm," she said. She was always going to call him to try to set the record straight, but she could never figure out the right way to do this.

The one time she tried, it was too late. Ten years had passed since she'd made her plea to him to help Apsara. The phone number she had for his office didn't work anymore, and it turned out there was no longer a company by that name. When she looked online, she saw it had been absorbed by a bigger company. No one at its main desk had ever heard of Gil.

She could call him at home, she decided. She wasn't doing anything his wife couldn't hear about. A grown woman could have a chat with an old friend, nothing incriminating in that.

I tried to explain this to the man I was seeing at the time. "I think she just wants him to think well of her. Everyone's like that, right? She won't ask for money again."

"I hope not," he said. "I mean, really."

I never took well to slurs against my family. He'd already been too confused that I had a sister I was close to but hadn't seen in over a decade. And I mentioned I had a father who was a ranger in the California desert. "What next?" he said.

"Too much for you, is it?" I said. "Where've you been in the world?" And I said some other things too.

He might've just been irritable because I was out of town more than he cared for, now that my work was having a boomlet, a little wave of attention. More people liked it. A film I did about women in nineteenth-century mill towns got very good write-ups. My big plan was to follow the topic overseas, shoot in Manchester and Leeds.

"I hope Gil knows how well you're doing," my mother said.

"Mom," I said, "nobody cares about documentaries."

"He'll be sorry he didn't invest when he could have."

"He's pining terribly."

Apsara had been going through a spell of not talking to us at all. For a while technology had allowed us to see her impish, mobile face on Skype or FaceTime, and she sent a video of her lovely, jumpy routines with the kids. She gave classes at a Y and at a preschool. But something had happened in the past two years. She'd grown harder to talk to, barely answered questions, was peevish and distracted. And then she disappeared again. We couldn't find her.

We couldn't tell if the cause was a no-good boyfriend or pharmaceuticals or worse. She wasn't so young anymore. Then my mother got a postcard from her saying *Just leave me alone for now.* My mother called to read it to me with tears in her voice. I was away; I was always away—this time in L.A., working on a film with Tracey. "She's too old for this crap," I said. "She can't be a baby forever. The woman is thirty-five fucking years old. You okay, Mom?"

It was a stupid question but the kind she always said yes to. That was how she was.

"It's too hard," my mother said. "I never knew it was going to be like this. Not when I was young and not later. Maybe nobody ever knows or they wouldn't get out of bed. It's too hard."

My mother found a phone number that might be Gil's, in an ancient Bell phone directory she'd never thrown out. On the Upper West Side, right? Worth a try. She left a brief message, and a woman called her back. The woman, Gil's wife, said she and Gil had been divorced for some time and she was sorry to have to tell Frankie this, but Gil had recently passed away. Just a few months before. "Stroke," she said.

"Oh!" my mother said.

My mother was sort of overwhelmed that the woman had bothered to call her back. "Well, it didn't seem right not to," the woman said. "You were an old friend?"

"I knew him before you did," my mother said. "Did he ever mention me?"

"I'm not sure," Gil's wife said. "I don't always remember names."

My mother spelled hers.

"Very nice to talk to you," the woman said.

"I should have called him long ago," my mother said to me. "Some things you shouldn't delay. You can't beg for forgiveness from someone who's dead."

"You can beg," I said. "But you can't get it. Maybe the begging is the point anyway."

I started to think that it was. Wasn't this my mother at her best, trying to make up for old heartlessness with a man she hardly knew anymore?

"We should all beg each other every minute," I said.

My mother laughed. We weren't going to go around doing that, not us. Not the types to walk around bowing our heads or kissing hems. But I was thinking of all the people I had wounded. A high count, and I was better than a lot of humans.

"I'm sorry," I said to my mother.

"Yes," my mother said. "Me too."

I wanted to beg Apsara. Where was she? And my father and more than a few old boyfriends. I had done all sorts of things to everyone.

Apsara surprised us, which she was always so good at doing. She was getting married! To Wilton, whom we knew from long ago. The news came in the form of a long phone call to my mom. No, she wasn't in Baltimore, what an idea, she was in Queens. That was where Wilton lived now. He'd become a lawyer; he worked in immigration law. Lot of work, not a lot of money.

My mother said, "This is so good!"

"Well, he's willing to join my crazy family," Apsara said.

We never asked how long they had been in Queens before deciding to get in touch.

How would we look to her now? My mother was arranging a gathering, a celebration, in her apartment on Ludlow Street, for all of us to meet again. Apsara would notice I was older around the middle and dyed my hair auburn and had a different style, a little snappier. Should I wear the big silver squiggle earrings? I'd just been through a long breakup and wouldn't be bringing anyone.

My mother squealed when they walked in, and I had to say, "Elvis has entered the building," while she hugged my sister to smithereens. My heart leaped up too. My sister was still a sprite-like person with spiky hair, but her face had grown bonier around it. She had stayed skinny and wiry from all that exercise with kids, which she still did at three different Y's. Wilton was balder but still cool in his black sport jacket. "The exiles return," I said.

Apsara giggled a lot, which we liked. We all talked about how the neighborhood had changed, nobody shooting drugs in doorways, how much better the city was doing, Miami too, how thrilled we were that Obama was president.

"I love Michelle," Apsara said.

Wilton said, "Nepal's still a mess, but we might go there for our honeymoon."

"Oh! I'm jealous," I said.

"Come along," Apsara said. A joke, but I loved it.

"Do you really remember it?" my mother said. "You were little."

"Well, I won't know where anything is," Apsara said.

I was thinking she must remember it fondly, if she was choosing to go now. I didn't think happiness could be a false memory, even if the particulars were all out of place.

Wilton said, "They have maps."

My mother was totally over the moon about the

wedding. "I could design the dresses," she said. "For you, Apsara—you'd look so pretty—and for me and Tara. I could sew them too, you know."

"What?" I said. Apsara and I were exchanging looks. We had to nip this one in the bud.

"I don't think so," Apsara said.

My mother saw our eye-rolling but chose not to complain. She was too thrilled to hold anything against my sister, who was home and alive and definitely in one piece (as we all turned out to be) and living close by, a mere subway ride away, and had given us a story that ended with a wedding.

7 / Ethan

NOTHING WAS THE SAME AFTER SAUL WAS GONE. This shouldn't have surprised me, but I imagined it differently. I'd grown attached to him, used to being around him more closely, more rawly than he would've wanted. I admired him, not because he handled the illness so well—sometimes he didn't—but because I understood by then who he was underneath it. He tried not to make things too difficult for Kirk or his sister or anyone taking care of him, and he had plenty of reasons to want to get Kirk's goat. He acted as if he didn't remember any of them.

I watched Kirk. He seemed to expect me to help, so I did. I thought, actually, that it drew us together to have these tasks. Getting Saul fed enough food that he liked, getting Saul settled tight in the bedsheets. I'd slip out the door not long after, and I'd go back to the life I had before I knew any of these people.

I wasn't there as much once the hospice aides showed up for their shifts. He got four hours a day covered by insurance, and what upright souls those health aides were, guys from ravaged parts of all continents, walking through the door in their dark cotton scrubs to do the awkward bits.

I got to know Saul before the last part. People said my helping my lover's ex-lover reminded them of the days of AIDS at its worst, when gay men rose to fine forms of team solidarity. Leukemia wasn't like that; anyone could get it without trying. We were just a party of three with shifting factions. Saul made cracks about Kirk behind his back, he'd imitate his favorite sayings, and we'd laugh knowingly together. We both loved him, but that was our own business.

In those days, when he was still interested in talking, Saul decided to say to me, "Do you believe in secrets?"

"Well," I said, "as a lawyer I have to have a tolerance for them. There's the attorney-client privilege thing. You're supposed to keep your mouth shut, as long as it's not about buried bodies. Famous case of lawyers getting in trouble for that."

Saul's secret was that he'd stolen a rare book. He had taken it out of the library's collection years ago just to look at—before the days when alarms shrieked at you, before computers logged every particle of matter—and he'd never brought it back. Nobody cared anymore, he was sure. And he wanted it sold now to leave a few bucks for Nadia. He had nothing else to will to her—any savings had long since been what they called "spent down" to let Medicaid kick in—and he really didn't want the book listed as his and taxed. But someone could sell it discreetly. I pointed out that lawyers had reason to balk at doing illegal things. "Maybe you know someone," he said. And he didn't want Kirk to know about it. He didn't want Kirk thinking poorly of him.

Kirk was three blocks away, buying ice cream. Did I want to see the book?

I could hardly believe what I saw. It was a first edition of Robert Louis Stevenson's *Treasure Island*, a book I'd loved intensely as a boy. It was just a brown clothbound book with gilt letters on the cover, but it had the author's signature, right there on the title page. I sort of swooned, though I knew that was silly of me. Robert Louis Stevenson! His handwriting. Cassell & Co., London, 1883.

"My mother used to read me his poems when I was little," I said. "She told me the pleasant land of counterpane was just a quilt. A word that's never come up since."

"He was sick all his life. TB probably."

"And she liked to say, 'Home is the sailor, home from sea.'"

"'And the hunter home from the hill.' That's his epitaph."

"You're kidding," I said. "We never knew that."

"It says, 'This be the verse you grave for me.' And they did; it's on his grave in Samoa."

We were both silent for a minute. "It's so vain," Saul said, "to pick something out ahead of time."

A bit of searching online turned up listings of similar copies (a few) selling at between fifteen thousand and twenty thousand dollars. Oh, there was the problem of its being stamped with the library's ID, but Saul had already written a letter on library stationery saying it was being deaccessioned. He had done this almost two years ago, when Kirk first talked about leaving him.

I thought my sister might know someone who collected priceless objects, who'd think nothing of writing a check for a venerable volume. No, I didn't want to drag my sister into this. I didn't want to be in it myself. What was I doing?

And wasn't *Treasure Island* a tale of how the lust for treasure made people betray and sabotage and murder one another? When I was eleven, my friend Mike and I used to go around chanting, "Fifteen men on the dead man's chest," that rousing gory anthem. Violent pirates, a boy's tale.

◆ ◆ ◆

I had no problem assuring Saul I would absolutely not tell Kirk about the book. It wasn't what I wanted to bring up anyway, in my snatched bits of time alone with the man who was still my boyfriend. We'd once had our long nights in that nice big apartment of his, making a royal progress from couch to bed to rug to bed and so on. After Saul was reinstalled on the premises, we had a different system. I'd send a Lyft to bring him down to my place—the whole length of Manhattan, Inwood to the Village—and we'd have our few hours to be a couple. We'd set the alarm so he wouldn't sleep too long; I loved watching him sleep. We never said, *This part won't last forever, we'll have more later, the future will be ours.* But we thought it; we held each other, knowing that time was passing along.

I had no idea, when I first flirted with Kirk, that anyone else was on the scene. We met on a train, of all places. I was going to see a friend in the Hudson Valley; he was on his way to an art directors' conference in Beacon. "Conferring means bullshitting," he said, in an archly charming way. We got to talking about the river outside the window, the glimmering, light-filled expanse of it. "I always think this is one of the great train rides," he said. I asked if he had traveled much—it turned out neither of us had really. We meant to. "Next year in Tahiti," he said.

"It's a date," I said.

Our first date was not in the South Seas but at a bar

with a view of the Manhattan skyline, very gorgeous at sunset, quite near my apartment in the West Village. He did tell me, over our mojitos, that he was sort of at the end of a relationship and they hadn't really stopped living together yet. Did that bother me?

"Nothing bothers me," I said, one of the bigger lies I've ever told. I thought if I was lighthearted, whatever we did would be easier for him. I would've said almost anything not to lose him before I had him. I was perfectly ready to make any bargains.

"He might be sick but it's not anything contagious," Kirk said. "Probably blood cancer."

He really said that. I wanted to ask him to repeat it but I didn't.

"It's hard to go home," he said. "It's pretty gloomy at home."

If he was trying to get my sympathy vote, it was entirely unnecessary. I didn't mind being his fling, his bad-boy hobby. I was well over forty and medium in looks; I hadn't been anyone's fling in years.

"He knows we're over," Kirk said.

I didn't want Kirk to say any more. Why did I think he was so great? I had reasons but they weren't real reasons. I was entirely gone over into wanting him.

And after we had our first time together, later that night but not too much later, I lay in bed floating on the immense certainty that I had, after all, a golden life. Better than I could have guessed. For however long. Luck had come to me; sometimes it does that.

I waited as long as I could before trying to explain Kirk to my mother. "It's very complicated," I told her. "You know how New York housing is."

"He's sick?" my mother said. "The guy he's leaving is sick?"

"He looks fine. You'd think he was fine if you saw him. He won't be alone. Kirk will keep helping."

"Did you ever read *David Copperfield*?"

I admitted not.

"He marries a pretty girl who turns out to be annoyingly childish and who conveniently falls ill. On her deathbed she tells him he's better off without her, and then he marries someone else. He has a vision of his first wife's spirit shining forth from his second wife's eyes to bless him. So he gets both at once. Double success. He's very pleased with himself."

Was she thinking of my father? Of his two Abbys?

"Men are no good," I said, though I was happy at the time.

"Watch out for yourself," she said.

✦ ✦ ✦

I would've liked to show my mother the *Treasure Island* with Stevenson's amazing signature. But it was Saul's secret, not mine. Kept for years, grown from a mistake to an ambition. I was there when Saul told his sister the tale of his purloined volume. Kirk was working late; Rachel and I were getting dinner together. We were doing dance moves to avoiding colliding in that tiny kitchen, goofing around, when Saul came to the doorway to tell her about this book he had. Was she alarmed that her brother the librarian—a man of moderate habits and intelligent judgments—had committed what was definitely grand larceny? "Oh, Saul," she said. "It's so nice of you to think of Nadia."

Nobody seemed to want to give it back to the library. The library had been balky about Saul's benefits and was not in good favor in this household—why give them money? Readers could read other copies, right?

And Saul had always been so penny-pinching, scolding Rachel and me when we splurged on gourmet treats to nourish him, as if he'd been keeping the book a secret from himself as well. Now he was changed overnight into the holder of a sizeable stash, don of the sickroom.

We all knew that thieves got caught when they tried to sell the goods. Did we know this from newscasts or from detective stories? Saul said it showed how useful crime fiction was. He was a lifelong fan.

"Maybe we can sell it overseas," Rachel said.

"I'm not sending it to your boyfriend in Cambodia," Saul said.

"Nobody has money in Cambodia," Rachel said.

"Singapore," I said.

A search showed there was only one rare bookstore in Singapore (for English-language books), an elegant spot— didn't we want a smaller and shadier outfit? Apparently, libraries were busy getting rid of their books and digitalizing everything, but rare books still had a market. Crazy rich Asians needed to buy things, I was sure. Not that I knew anything about any of this. But there had to be sneaky private dealers of antique items in that city, if a person knew how to find them. Could a Chinese-speaker help me? Or was that a whole other world? Maybe I'd go to Singapore myself.

And then we got distracted. Saul took a turn for the worse. He reported pain—anyone could see it cast its shadow over whatever expression his face had—and after too many bad days, he was properly drugged so he could fall into off-and-on napping. Sometimes I helped get him sitting up in bed to let Kirk feed him from a tray. Once he was up, I was no longer wanted in the room. The plans for getting cash for the book seemed like a frivolous and bizarre fantasy. A nutty idea very far from the heart of the matter.

It was too long, this stage when he was stretched on the vicious rack of his cancer, but afterward he seemed to have faded out just like that, without giving us a chance to get enough of him before he was gone. And the health aides were there in those last weeks, lifting and hoisting and helping, more adept and less afraid than we were.

Kirk asked if I didn't mind not going to the funeral. "It's too weird for me to bring a date," he said. "You know what I mean."

I thought I could sit in the back but he didn't think so.

"We'll talk later," he said. "Don't nag me. Now is not the time."

"You're banning me?" I said. "What is this about?"

"I'm not getting into it now."

"You're the one who decides who gets to mourn Saul? He would hate this, he would totally hate it."

"Don't tell me about Saul," he said. "You have no right."

"I have no fucking rights of any kind," I said, and that was the end of that conversation.

The service was at a Jewish funeral home in the Bronx that his sister found; the prayers would've been familiar to me. I thought of coming anyway, but I was ashamed to bring any feuding into such a place. I hated not being there. I never would've let Saul down by just skipping it, as if I were too busy. I sent his sister a note by email, to say I was honoring Kirk's request.

The funeral must've had speeches extolling and loving Saul and granting him his new sanctity as one of the dead. I knew what they'd say. In Kirk's case, as he sat in the first row, all of it had the further effect of reminding him (over and over, with each speech) how much he regretted his collusion with me. How very much. We'd gone into it together, our long, impatient betrayal of Saul.

"You always told me nothing *bothered* you, why didn't it?" he couldn't wait to ask me. "What was the matter with you?" He said this over the phone, four days after the funeral. I'd had to keep calling at different times before I reached him.

"It's better if you just don't say anything," he said. "I don't think I could stand to hear it."

This was Kirk, the prize I'd been waiting for. I'd gotten everything wrong, hadn't I?

"I know you can argue, you're a lawyer, but don't," he said. "Just don't, okay?"

"Maybe we should talk at a later time," I said.

"I don't think so. I really do not."

There was a pause, and what was I listening for next?

"Did you hear me?" Kirk said. How eager he was for me to disappear. The sign of his corruption.

"Well," I said. "Fuck. That's it then."

My sister, Allyson, said, "I never liked him," though she'd only met him once and they'd gotten quite hilarious talking about some high-end restaurant.

My mother said, "People get over these things." She meant it as good news.

"And he made me miss Saul's funeral," I said. It was demoralizing to long for someone I was on my way to despising. "Not that funerals are so great."

"In Thailand," my mother said, "everybody walks past the covered body and they pour perfumed water on the corpse's right hand—you know, for purifying—and they ask forgiveness for any quarrels they had."

"I never quarreled with Saul," I said.

It was true we'd had disputes about why he refused to eat something he'd just asked for, and always we had our silent subterranean quarrel about who got to have Kirk. Saul had won that battle and he didn't even know.

✦ ✦ ✦

I dreamed over and over about Saul. In the dreams I was always thrilled to see him, out of the blue like that. *Hey, Saul. There you are.* He looked much better than he had before he died, not withered and skeletal anymore. In one dream, he was complaining that he wanted a warmer sweater, was that too much to ask, and I was looking all over and couldn't find the one he wanted anywhere.

Was he a ghost?

And I dreamed of Kirk too, who was definitely not a ghost. In one dream he was ravenous for sex. In another he was locking me into a large metal trunk, no matter how I resisted. In another he was baking a cake that burned and then something else happened I couldn't remember. My sleep life was not helping me.

I was moving through the days, putting one foot in front of the other, trying to focus at work (we had a libel case that would've been interesting had I been interested) and letting friends give their well-meant and patroniz-ing pep talks, when I got a message from Saul's sister, Rachel. It was about the copy of *Treasure Island*, which she still had.

At first, she wrote, *Nadia wanted to keep it, to have some-thing of his, but she has his Buddha and a bunch of other things.*

Now she's thinking about her future. Maybe we can meet and you can help me review possibilities.

I could not advise her to do anything illegal. Reviewing was perhaps something else. I was really very glad that she wanted to see me.

I met Rachel in some café she liked on Eighth Avenue in the Fifties. We hugged fondly, which we'd actually never done before. When I said how sorry I was about Saul, she said that the one having the most trouble now was Nadia.

"She's a good kid," I said.

In fact, Nadia hated me for a long time. If she saw me in the elevator, she'd turn her head and look elsewhere. She got used to me once I was around more, doing tasks for Saul. We'd been known to laugh at the same joke. She herself was not that helpful, except for reading to Saul sometimes. He liked that.

"She's had a lot of instability in her life," Rachel said. "And I was sort of planning to go away in a month. To Cambodia, just a couple of weeks. I'm not thrilled about leaving her on her own."

"I can look in on her," I said. "Take her to dinner, if you think she'd go with me."

"You can try," Rachel said. "Thank you. She loves Mexican food. Well, you've seen that."

"Glad to do it," I said.

"Have you ever been to Singapore?"

"Not me," I said.

"I'm going to stop there on the way back from Cambodia. My friend Bud knows someone there. To get the book sold."

"It's supposed to be a great city."

"Do you know—I thought you would know—is there a limit to how much cash you can bring back to this country?"

"Ten thousand. Otherwise you have to report it."

"What can they do to you?"

"Well, they can take it from you. There could be fines or civic or criminal penalties. It's not really my area, you know that."

"So we'd have to split it," Rachel said. "Bud could carry half. He'd have to come back with me. Or visit me later."

"If you trust him," I said.

She looked startled at this. I'd offended her.

"Sorry," I said. "I've read too much about men plotting mutiny to get the treasure map."

"I guess," she said.

You could say, if you wanted to, that a dying man's last wish was being carried out in this planned excursion to the underbelly of Singapore. Rachel undoubtedly saw it as a mission of honor.

If her friend didn't know what the hell he was doing, there were risks even I'd read about. Transactions with "unlawful societies" (what we would call the Mob) in

Singapore were punishable by strokes of the cane as well as prison. They didn't do it to women.

Her friend surely knew all that. I said, "Have a great vacation."

My dreams got weirder. In one I was setting up a deal with Saul: if I bought him a new apartment, a pricey one in Chelsea, with a balcony overlooking the High Line, he'd get Kirk to come back to me, he'd talk him into it. "I can do it," he said. "People listen to me now." On a different night, I dreamed that Saul and I left a bar together and strolled along the river toward a deserted mansion that I knew was the house of the dead. No lights on. I walked him to the gabled front door and started to go inside, but I didn't get further than the black hallway before I woke up. A friend at work said his Chinese grandmother would say it was actually auspicious to dream about your own death. It could mean a rise in prosperity or that you were about to start a new stage of life. "Hey," I said, "I'm ready." The dream had not felt that cheerful to me, but I wasn't about to argue against any grandmothers.

I spoke to Rachel once more before she left, and she talked about Nadia, how outraged she still was. "She's mad about what life is," Rachel said. "That nothing lasts, that no one does. That we lose everything. She doesn't like it. It was okay when the Buddha said it but not now." Essentially Nadia and I were on the same page.

I called her the day after Rachel took off for Cambodia. She was very surprised to hear my voice. "Ethan?" she said.

I said I had a big hunger for tacos al pastor and I knew she liked that kind of thing so maybe she would keep me company. The place had good elote too.

"Really good?" she said. "Not under-grilled?"

She was wearing stagey eye makeup, dark feral outlines, when I got to the restaurant. Why was I doing this? My connection to these people was Kirk, who was lost and out of sight.

"The menu looks so typical," Nadia said.

But we did better after that. I said I'd heard Mexican cuisine was very regional and I asked if she ever thought about going to Mexico. "I wanted to take Saul to Jamaica," she said. "He didn't want to go."

"You know the only place I've ever been," I said, "is Iceland. My mother's idea. We ended up going in summer, when it stays light at night, this dreamy twilight. I loved that."

"Nothing wrong with Jamaica. He can't go anywhere now."

I didn't believe in an afterlife, but I knew most of Asia believed in reincarnation. What did she think of that?

"I want to talk to him," she said. "That doesn't help."

Nothing was going to help; we had to help ourselves. Right now I was no better at this than Nadia.

She was eating enough, which I took as a good sign. "I hated all the hypocrisy at the funeral," she said, chewing.

"People don't know what to do," I said. "They can't always say what they mean."

"So when can they? When do they stop lying?"

She had me on that one. "Don't ask me now. I'll remember eventually."

I felt terrible being the cynical old guy just when she was fallen into darkness. "No, you won't," she said, with a snide little lilt.

I never should've taken her anywhere. I was the wrong person.

"With the light always on in Iceland," Nadia said, "don't they get confused about where they are in the day?"

"They have skills we don't have," I said. "That's what travel is."

"How do you know if you've only been to one place?"

"Forget I said anything."

What this meal was doing was baring my despair. It reminded me how old I was, how limited my stock of chances was. It was a cruel and dark time for Nadia, but anyone could see she had a long string of hearts ahead of her.

"I can't believe Rachel really wanted to go to Cambodia," she said. "That guy brainwashed her."

"I don't think so," I said.

"You know how long it takes to get there? And what it costs?"

I finished my ear of corn. "How's school?" I said.

"Kirk is an asshole," Nadia said, to be nice to me.

I sent an email to Rachel to tell her I'd seen Nadia. Rachel wrote, *I'm liking Phnom Penh—great palace, temples, food. But even when I was young, I don't think I ever visited a place this poor. And we think we have problems. Bud is a good guide.*

Nice to hear she was getting along with Bud. Maybe old boyfriends were a good idea. Tony, my ex, had moved to Washington, D.C., which was not that far away. But didn't I know better than to repeat old mistakes? Of course, he might have changed.

My friend Mike used to have theories about reincarnation, when we were teenagers. "Can't kill energy," he would say. Did anyone want to be reborn just as reordered elements released into the ether? (This was Nadia's point too.) What was the good of continuing in another form?

Mike said, "We get too stuck in particularity. Think big." He had the temperament of a brainy kid. Now when I couldn't sleep, I tried to remember what that meant, thinking big.

I was doing better, I thought, when I suddenly got a phone call from Rachel, late at night. "Are you back already?" I said. She was not back. She was still in Phnom Penh, and she had just discovered, trying to withdraw from an ATM, that she had no money in her checking account. She tried other ATMs, other banks, but it looked like someone in Cambodia had gotten into the account—a person who'd been in line after her at a cash machine, or hovered near her at a local bank. People had ways. In a Third World country, the thirty-five hundred in the account was life-changing, more than twice the median income. She'd been trying to let Nadia know, since Nadia used the card too. But there was no way to get hold of Nadia. Not answering texts, emails, phone calls. Had I seen her lately? I had not.

And then the bank at home, Rachel said, told her that the withdrawals had been from New York banks. A whole sequence of withdrawals over a few days. A customer-service woman at the bank read her the locations. In the West Forties, where the apartment was; in Chelsea, where Nadia's school was.

"So Nadia took the money," she said. "Mystery solved."

"Oh, shit," I said.

Couldn't Nadia's card just have been stolen? And then the thief somehow figured out the password, like a safe-cracker listening to the dial? A genius techie.

"Can you see if you can find her?" Rachel said.

I found her at school. I knew from Rachel that she had an eleven o'clock class, and I spent some of my lunch break waiting outside the main FIT entrance on West Twenty-Seventh Street for her to exit. I must have looked like a stalker, standing with my coffee while all those hiply dressed kids, girls in draped layers and boys with zany glasses, swarmed by me. She was wearing the same funny plaid dress she'd worn to dinner, definitely not in disguise.

"Hey, Nadia!" I said.

"Ethan?" she said.

She hadn't run away with the cash to Paris, or to the beaches of Jamaica either. Maybe she never took a cent.

"I can't get in touch with Rachel," I said. "Have you heard from her? Is she okay?"

"She's fine," Nadia said. "Maybe she doesn't want to talk to you."

"I was going to send her money. She's run out of cash and she's stranded. I'm worried now."

"She's fine," Nadia said. "She has that Bud guy."

"Let's hope he hasn't deserted her. Not having money is serious."

"Excuse me," Nadia said, to two young women I now saw were with her. "I have to talk to this person."

She led me to the corner of the street, away from the crowd. "Rachel has charge cards," she said. "You don't even know her and you're all worried about her. No one is worried about me."

"Oh, I'm worried," I said. "I see where you're going. I'm a lawyer."

"I have a crap father and now I have you too?"

"Rachel loves you," I said. "Maybe you can send her some money. Do you have savings?"

"Me?" she said. "Maybe a little."

"Since you know where she is," I said. "And I don't. That would help. I'm sure she'd be very grateful."

"She doesn't care what I do."

"Oh, please." I sighed, which meant, *Listen to yourself,* and we left it at that.

I worked in civil litigation, but Tony, my ex, did matrimonial law, and he used to tell me that people filing for divorce were always trying to collect, in the form of money, payment for what could never be paid for. How literal they were, listing their highly graphic complaints. The suffering was real, the money was real, but the relation between the two was a delusion. Which the world was full of. Love and money were always twisted and tangled, always mistaken for each other. Nadia had been doing so much better before Saul got really sick. She was probably angry at the Buddha too.

I thought of her chanting to the Buddha for Saul. She did it sometimes in Kirk's apartment. *May he live with ease.* Kirk and I, the nonbelievers, would look at each other with something between amusement and heartbreak. How enchanted I was with Kirk then; the drama of Saul had become something precious to me, because of him. I'd go home from those evenings, after our not-too-lingering kiss at the door, with a feeling like joy in wait.

Probably love always has its ironies. As a child I had been very shocked to learn that genitals were involved in adult romance—it made no sense, when I was five. So I'd lived all these years with the comic tyrannies of the body, their ungainliness and majesty. Whatever wild sweetness I'd had with Kirk no longer seemed glorious, but I missed it all the time. Every minute.

The money didn't all come back into Rachel's account but most of it did. When Rachel looked at her balance onscreen again, it was up to twenty-eight hundred. She phoned me late at night to tell me. "What did you do?" she said. "A miracle."

"We spoke in secret code," I told her. "Like pirates. Well, not code, really, but veiled allusions. We liked it."

We weren't passing off any black spots to Long John Silver on torn Bible paper but we had our understanding, we were in league. So it felt. But who knew what Nadia would think of to do next?

"And I thought it was just some poor Cambodian," Rachel said. "Thank God I didn't accuse anyone. It shows how wrong you can be."

"Things are okay otherwise? You have enough?"

"I thought Nadia was done with all that. It's not like I get a huge salary. She knows that. I didn't see this coming. I should have but I didn't want to."

"Has she ever taken anything before?"

"I don't want to talk about it."

"She'll be all right," I said. "You going to Angkor Wat?"

"I don't even care anymore," she said. "But we're going."

I told my mother the whole story about Nadia stealing. Being my mother, she was full of praise for my cleverness with her. We were having brunch at her house, wolfing down bagels with the kippered salmon I liked.

"After all that Rachel's done for her," I said.

"Pretty usual," my mother said. She had taught middle school long enough to have seen everything. Changing fads in lunacy and disruption and inventive adolescent cruelty had passed under her gaze for years.

Did that make her calmer, not to be surprised each time?

"Yes," she said. "In my case it did."

It made me glad to hear it. Tony used to say that my mother was much less ignorant than most people. He meant exactly this. She tended to know what mattered and what didn't.

"She's not the worst, this Nadia," my mother said.

In the early days, Kirk used to take me for walks in Inwood Park, which was quite a spectacular park, an expanse of radiant nature, foresty hillsides and a pond on which ducks swam and white egrets hovered in the distance, a place entirely unknown to me before then. "I knew you'd like it," he said. I took its remarkable vistas as a sign of Kirk's greatness, as new lovers do. It was not that far from the apartment, so I should not have been so wounded when in later days Saul spoke of the great picnics he and Kirk had had there, the beautiful trails they got lost on. I hated hearing about the tulip trees. But I pretended I had never seen the place. "It's near here?" I said. I could do that much for Saul.

I went to walk there now, on a late Sunday afternoon when I had no business in the neighborhood. It was winter by this time, though the park was still pretty, even in its bareness. I told myself I was saying goodbye to all this, though I probably hoped to see Kirk slip out from behind an oak tree.

I saw a baby raccoon up a tree, actually, which was exciting. A masked hoodlum—I wanted to take a picture, as if he were a fabulous tourist discovery. This was like travel for a New Yorker, wasn't it? I got the back of him, his furry behind with its striped tail, before he moved. My mother would like that shot.

My sister, Allyson, said, "You're doing so well, I think. After the breakup, I mean." I was furious at her for this. I thought it was an insult to my sorrow, to the true rottenness of losing Kirk, who was better than anyone would say now. And an extra insult to my mourning for Saul, which she didn't know that much about. "Thank you," I said, just to get the whole issue off the table.

My sister meant well. Everyone wanted me back the way I was. Which was not what I even wanted.

✦ ✦ ✦

It wasn't that long before Rachel was back in New York. "It was a fantastic trip," she said on the phone. "I know it didn't sound like that at certain times but it was." She had a souvenir for me; we would have brunch, yes?

She arrived wrapped in two wool scarves over her coat. "It's hard to get used to winter again," she said, untwining herself. "You wouldn't believe how hot Singapore was."

"New York must seem like a mirage," I said. It was January and twenty degrees outside, with some really mean winds.

"It's all a mirage," she said, happily.

This was a good thing?

"And Singapore's not all fancy, like people think. I was in a hawker center eating fried dough for breakfast three days ago."

"Did you sell *Treasure Island?*"

"It's a long story," she said.

Bud, her friend, was somehow friends with a Brit who helped run a community addiction-recovery center (lot of gambling addicts, he said) in an eastern edge of Singapore. He couldn't introduce Bud to anyone, not directly, but he could show him who to talk to. They went to a coffee place nearby and he pointed to a table of old Chinese men in the corner playing backgammon. That is, two of them were playing; the others were watching and waiting. The players looked like old men at a game anywhere—could've been dominoes, poker, craps—very intent, not speaking, lost in strategy. The guy they needed to talk to was the clean-shaven one in the dark blue shirt, with a scar on his cheek.

"We were not invisible in the café," Rachel said. "Every single person noticed us. I had no idea how to read that room. And I had to think, *We're out of our depth here.* Bud was saying he knew how to handle it, not to worry. And if he didn't know? I didn't want him showing off, risking our necks or whatever. What would Nadia do if I never came back? I told him I'd changed my mind. Which I really, really had."

"He was okay with this?"

"Bud was insulted. He didn't say much except, 'You're sure?' His friend had already left; I knew he'd be embarrassed to have to tell him the whole thing was for nothing. And when we were walking around on the street, he said, 'Why did we bother to come here then?' I had no answer."

Not the story I expected.

"But you know what? He got over it. By the evening he'd decided that Singapore was a great place to visit, this was a good accident. We had fun. Temples, mosques, dancing in the street, Malay food, Indian food. It's much more fun there than people say."

"You still have the book?"

"I have it on a shelf next to other things he liked—an ice cream dish and some detective novels by Dashiell

Hammett. Sort of a shrine to Saul. Nadia can decide what to do with it when she's older."

"Keep it safe."

"I had her read it in paperback. She loved Long John Silver."

"Freedom is a great thing."

"Yes," she said. "He gets away in the end, doesn't he? Escapes from the ship taking him to prison. He and his parrot."

"Would Saul have liked his shrine?"

"He liked being loved. And for us, it reminds us that love is not in vain."

I had spent the last few months thinking that it was. "Didn't the Buddha think so?"

"I think that's a misreading," Rachel said. "We have to ask Nadia. She's been on Buddhist webs again—she's the expert."

Nadia was an expert on anything? They must be getting along better.

"We had a talk," Rachel admitted, rolling her eyes. She could joke about forgiveness. "A really long talk."

"Think you'll ever go to Cambodia again?"

"Oh, yes," she said. "Often, if I can."

✦　✦　✦

Rachel had brought me a souvenir of Angkor Wat. It was a refrigerator magnet of molded plastic that showed four women dancing—they had bare breasts and very narrow waists and wore fabulous towering headdresses as they crooked their knees and raised their elegant arms in chorus. Rachel said they were *apsaras*, spirits of clouds and waters, carved all over the Angkor temples.

I still had it in my coat pocket when I went to visit my mom a few days later.

"She brought you a girly picture?" my mother said.

"They're guardians," I said. "That's what she told me. They protect the king of the gods by seducing his enemies."

I wondered as I said it whether I had seemed to Rachel to be in need of seductive backup. Maybe I had already slept with all my enemies.

Well, that sounded bitter. Could I not think of Kirk as a mere deluded human? Dreaming in too many ways about his right to escape?

"It's very nice that she thought of you," my mother said.

My mother was afraid I was going to keep getting myself into miserable love catastrophes. She always wanted to hear I had friends.

"Rachel liked Cambodia," I said. "Thinks about going again."

My father never went to Cambodia, but my mother had drawerfuls of the trinkets and fabrics he brought back to her from other places. She still wore all the terrific silk scarves, which she liked and chose not to be negatively sentimental about. Brocades and batiks. She had her own apportionment of feelings, my mother. She lit a Yahrzeit candle on the yearly anniversary of my father's death, no matter, she said, what her opinions were.

My mother was someone with plenty of strong opinions, but they were lesser to her around big deals like death. People all over the world set out candles for the dead, the flames standing in for souls. (Buddhists didn't believe in souls, Nadia had told me. They lit candles anyway.) My mother had plenty of reasons not to wish my father well, but every year she bought that wax-filled glass at the kosher market. It was what a serious person did, took a longer view. If my father, wherever he was, was not grateful, she didn't take it personally. She thought that question was a mistake. She lit the flame just before sundown out of a larger project.

I was with her one night, watching her light it in the kitchen. Would my father have cared that he was being honored on the windowsill over the sink? He'd be glad enough, I thought, and surprised too, if surprise is available to someone on the other side of this life. He would hardly have recognized the kitchen, which had been redone since his time. I was remembering when we all used to slide on the linoleum in our socks. My father did fancy loops and skids. He was a fun dad when he wanted to be. I did wonder (not for the first time) how my mother came to choose him. I of all people should've understood it, the sunny opacity that love can induce. They'd met in a line outside a phone booth (no more of those), in another century. I knew that century, I wasn't young either. (I used to taunt Kirk for being older, another thing to regret.) How matter-of-fact my mother was as she struck the match, how excellent it was for me to see her.

Acknowledgments

Once again, I am deeply grateful for the superb advice and counsel of my dear friend Myra Goldberg. I send heartfelt thanks for the astute and eagle-eyed attention of Chuck Wachtel and for the precious conversation of Kathleen Hill. I want to thank my wonderful editor, Dan Smetanka, and everyone at Counterpoint, and my remarkable agent, Geri Thoma.

Portions of this novel have appeared previously in magazines. Chapter 1 appeared as "Secrets of Happiness" in *The Southern Review*, Chapter 2 appeared as "Love and Money" in *The Yale Review*, Chapter 3 appeared as "Freedom from Delusion" in *Sun*, Chapter 4 appeared as "Freedom from Want" in *Tin House*, Chapter 5 appeared as "Fields of Empire" in *The Missouri Review*, and Chapter 7 appeared as "The Overland Trail" in *The Southern Review*. I owe special thanks to Andrea Morrison.

© Shari Diamond

JOAN SILBER is the author of nine books of fiction. Her last book, *Improvement*, was the winner of the National Book Critics Circle Award and the PEN/Faulkner Award and was listed as one of the year's best books by *The Washington Post*, *The Wall Street Journal*, *Newsday*, *The Seattle Times*, and *Kirkus Reviews*. Her previous book, *Fools*, was long-listed for the National Book Award and was a finalist for the PEN/Faulkner Award. Other works include *The Size of the World*, finalist for the Los Angeles Times Book Prize for Fiction, and *Ideas of Heaven*, finalist for the National Book Award and The Story Prize. She lives in New York, has taught at Sarah Lawrence College, and teaches in the Warren Wilson MFA program. Find out more at joansilber.net.